Humbug

by

John Wooten

SAMUEL FRENCH

FOUNDED 1830

NEW YORK HOLLYWOOD LONDON TORONTO

SAMUELFRENCH.COM

ISBN 978-0-573-66279-9   Printed in U.S.A.   #10959

IMPORTANT BILLING AND CREDIT REQUIREMENTS

All producers of *HUMBUG* *must* give credit to the Author of the Play in all programs distributed in connection with performances of the Play, and in all instances in which the title of the Play appears for the purposes of advertising, publicizing or otherwise exploiting the Play and/or a production. The name of the Author *must* appear on a separate line on which no other name appears, immediately following the title and *must* appear in size of type not less than fifty percent of the size of the title type.

"HUMBUG was originally produced at Premiere Stages, an Equity theatre in residence at Kean University"

PRODUCTION INFORMATION

HUMBUG was originally produced by Premiere Stages at Kean University, a professional Equity theatre in Union, NJ.

Producer: Lindsay Gambini
Associate Producer: Elizabeth Coen
Director: John Wooten
Set Designer: Bill Moytka
Lighting Designer: Brant Thomas Murray
Costume Designer: Karen Lee Hart
Sound Designer: Bryan Pekarek
Stage Manager: Rosie Goldman
Casting Director: Carol Hanzel

The December cast included:

ELEANOR SCROOGE	Rita Rehn
BOBBIE CRATCHIT	Jordan Simmons
CAROLER #1/TESS/PRESENT	Andrea Bianchi
CAROLER #2/TUG/BILL	Shabazz Green
CAROLER #3/ELLIE/LISA	Susanna Harris
CAROLER #4/PAST/JUAN	Jon Hoche
JOHN/ROBERT/GRAVEDIGGER	Jason Marr
PHIL	Matthew DeCapua
SARAH	Lacey Jones
BEN	Jeff Ronan
MARLEY/BENSON	Allen Lewis Rickman
YOUNG PHIL/TIMMY	Tommy Kouten
CARLA/NELLIE	Emma Gordon
FUTURE	Robert Cole

CHARACTERS

ELEANOR SCROOGE: 40s; female; attractive; corporate; sharp; sarcastic; intimidating.

BOBBIE CRATCHIT: 30s; female; a good soul; loyal; mother; Scrooge's assistant.

CAROLER #1/PRESENT: 30s; female, exceptionally adept character actress; small; requires cockney accent; sings well.

CAROLER #2/ELLIE/LISA: 20s; female; attractive; plays Young Scrooge; versatile actress required; sings well.

CAROLER #3/TUG/BILL/BENSON: 30s; male; versatile actor required; sings well.

CAROLER #4/PAST/JUAN: 20s; male; handsome; strong comic and versatile actor required; sings well.

BEN/JACOB MARLEY/GRAVEDIGGER: 40s-50s; male; strong comic and versitile actor required.

PHIL: 20s; male; Scrooge's nephew; good-natured and likable.

JOHN/ROBERT/FUTURE: 30s; male; tall; handsome; charming; strong comic and versatile actor required.

SARAH/NURSE/NELLIE: 20s; female; strong comic and versatile actress required.

TESS/CARLA: LATE 20s; female; plays Eleanor's sister; versatile actress required.

YOUNG PHIL/TIMMY: 9; male; plays Eleanor's nephew and Bobbie's son; stage experience required.

TIME
The Present, Christmas Eve

SETTING
A Wall Street Office Suite, on the 16th Floor

Allowed changes to script: The lines refering to Past's ethnicity can be altered should an Asian actor not be cast in the role. The height of Past can also be changed to represent the actual height of the actor playing the role.

For Andrea
The funniest gal I know

(Lights rise on **ELEANOR SCROOGE**'s *corporate office suite on the 16th floor of a Manhattan High-Rise.* **ELEANOR** *is in her office working frantically in front of her computer.* **BOBBIE CRATCHIT** *sits at her desk in the reception area. In front of her desk are a group of* **CAROLERS** *enthusiastically singing "God Rest Ye Merry Gentlemen."* **BOBBIE** *and the carolers are bundled up in coats. The windows are frosted with ice [from the inside]. The windows in* **ELEANOR**'s *office are covered with blinds. A coat rack with* **ELEANOR**'s *long black coat is behind her desk against the upstage wall.* **BOBBIE** *smiles at the carolers, enjoying their rendition.* **ELEANOR** *looks up from her computer screen and watches the* **CAROLERS** *a moment through her door. She looks back at the screen, mumbling to herself. The* **CAROLERS** *continue, singing more loudly.* **ELEANOR** *rises from her desk and crosses to the door. She watches the carolers for a moment, smiles, and then slams her door with full force. Frightened, the* **CAROLERS** *abruptly stop singing. They look at* **BOBBIE**. **BOBBIE** *smiles weakly at the carolers, a bit embarrassed.)*

BOBBIE. Maybe a bit softer.

(The **CAROLERS** *smile. They gather around* **BOBBIE** *and begin to sing again, in little more than a whisper.* **ELEANOR** *slowly looks up from her computer screen. She listens. She then yells into her intercom that connects to* **BOBBIE**'s *desk.)*

ELEANOR. Fire!

(The **CAROLERS** *leap away from the intercom and scramble toward the door.)*

BOBBIE. Wait!

(**BOBBIE** *crosses to the door, carrying her purse.* **ELEANOR** *laughs – quite pleased with herself – and goes back*

to her computer screen.)

BOBBIE. I'm sorry.

*(**BOBBIE** digs through her tattered purse, trying to find change. She digs out all that she has – a few rumpled dollar bills and coins – and gives them to the **CAROLERS**. She has nothing left to give the last **CAROLER** so she shakes his hand. The **CAROLERS** say "Thank you," "Merry Christmas," "Happy Holidays" etc. as they exit. Frazzled, **BOBBIE** closes the door and leans her back against it. She sighs. She crosses back to her desk and begins to stuff a great deal of files into her large, tattered briefcase. **ELEANOR** talks into the intercom to **BOBBIE**.)*

ELEANOR. I need the memo on the Misslehouse takeover, Cratchit.

BOBBIE. Which takeover, Ma'am?

ELEANOR. Misslehouse!

BOBBIE. I haven't proofed it.

ELEANOR. It's alright. Too many cooks spoil the broth.

*(**BOBBIE** begins to pack files into the large briefcase)*

And don't even think of packing up until that document is on my desk.

BOBBIE. *(Into intercom.)* Can I turn up the thermostat a bit?

ELEANOR. *(Into intercom.)* I already turned it up once. If you wanted to bake, you should have stayed in L.A.

BOBBIE. *(Into intercom.)* But there's ice on the inside of the windows.

ELEANOR. *(Into intercom.)* You're on the 16th floor, Cratchit. What do you expect to see?

BOBBIE. *(Into intercom.)* Just up to 60?...50?

ELEANOR. *(Into intercom.)* What is the most important thing I've taught you over the past six years?

BOBBIE. *(Into intercom.)* Hell hath no fury like a woman scorned.

ELEANOR. *(Into intercom.)* What else? More relevant to your request.

(**BOBBIE** *begins to grab Post-its she has pasted in various places on and around her computer.*)

BOBBIE. *(Into intercom.)* Fools rush in where angels fear to tread.

(**ELEANOR** *sighs into the intercom.*)

You dance with what brung ya'?

ELEANOR. *(Into intercom.)* I said relevant!

BOBBIE. *(Into intercom.)* Complainers drain, solvers reign.

ELEANOR. *(Into intercom.)* Right. And which do you strive to be, Cratchit? A complainer or a solver?

BOBBIE. *(Into intercom.)* I wasn't complaining, Ma'am, I only…

ELEANOR. *(Into intercom.)* Enough. Buy a thicker coat, Roberta.

BOBBIE. *(Into intercom.)* Yes, Ma'am.

(**BOBBIE** *begins humming a Christmas carol.* **ELEANOR** *listens at the door.*)

ELEANOR. *(Into intercom.)* Are those screaming mimis still here?

BOBBIE. *(Into intercom.)* The carolers? No.

ELEANOR. *(Into intercom.)* Oh, god. Were you singing again?

BOBBIE. *(Into intercom.)* Humming.

ELEANOR. *(Into intercom.)* Well, don't. Singing, humming, or any musical sound coming from you is not a good idea, Cratchit. A closed mouth catches no flies.

BOBBIE. *(Into intercom.)* Yes, Ma'am.

ELEANOR. *(Into intercom.)* Did your husband encourage you to make that noise?

BOBBIE. *(Into intercom.)* No, Ma'am.

ELEANOR. *(under her breath)* I didn't think so. Probably what drove him away.

(**BOBBIE** *hears her.* **BOBBIE** *grabs her purse, keys, and picture frames on her desk and heads for the door.* **ELEANOR** *realizes she may have gone too far [even for her].*)

Alright. You can turn the heat up. To 55...Cratchit? You there?

BOBBIE. *(Into intercom.)* Uh...I am. Yes, Ma'am. Thank you.

*(**BOBBIE** considers. She crosses to the thermostat. She turns it up. She puts her things back on the desk and sticks her tongue out at **ELEANOR**'s closed door. She gives a raspberry, makes gyrations toward **ELEANOR**'s door, etc.* **JOHN** *enters and watches* **BOBBIE**. **BOBBIE** *turns and sees him. She stops her movements, embarrassed.)*

JOHN. Good evening.

BOBBIE. Good evening.

JOHN. Is Ms. Scrooge in?

*(**BOBBIE** crosses to her desk.)*

BOBBIE. Can I help you with...?

JOHN. I need to speak with her about my company.

BOBBIE. Do you have an appointment?

JOHN. It's urgent.

BOBBIE. I'm sorry, but she requires an appointment for anyone she sees.

*(**BOBBIE** checks her scheduling book.)*

I could fit you in next Friday if...

JOHN. It can't wait.

*(**BOBBIE** looks at **JOHN**.)*

Please.

*(**BOBBIE** considers. She reaches over to the intercom.)*

BOBBIE. Your name?

JOHN. John Misslehouse.

BOBBIE. Excuse me?

JOHN. Misslehouse.

*(**BOBBIE** has a pained look on her face.)*

BOBBIE. One moment.

*(**BOBBIE** picks up the phone on the intercom rather than*

pushing the intercom button. The phone rings in **ELEANOR**'s *office.* **ELEANOR** *snatches up the phone.)*

ELEANOR. What are you doing? You know I hate the phone.

*(***ELEANOR** *slams down the receiver.* **BOBBIE** *smiles weakly at* **JOHN** *and crosses to the door to* **ELEANOR**'s *office, taking the Misslehouse memo with her.* **BOBBIE** *taps lightly on the door)*

What?!

BOBBIE. *(Entering the office and closing the door behind her)* John Misslehouse is here to see you.

ELEANOR. Who?

BOBBIE. *(Showing* **ELEANOR** *the memo.)* From Misslehouse Industrials.

ELEANOR. *(Lighting up with a smile.)* Perfect. Lay it on him.

BOBBIE. But...are you sure?

ELEANOR. Shall I compose another one? For you?

BOBBIE. No, Ma'am. It's just...

ELEANOR. Give him the letter, Cratchit.

BOBBIE. It's Christmas Eve.

ELEANOR. Do it!

*(***BOBBIE** *slowly walks back into the reception area. She smiles weakly at* **JOHN**. **ELEANOR** *crosses to her door and opens it a crack so she can watch* **BOBBIE** *and* **JOHN**. *She smiles with anticipation.)*

BOBBIE. Ms. Scrooge apologizes that she is unable to see you. But...well...she asked me to give you this.

*(***BOBBIE** *hands* **JOHN** *the document.* **JOHN** *reads it. He looks at* **BOBBIE** *in disbelief and then charges toward* **ELEANOR**'s *office.* **ELEANOR** *rushes back to her chair.* **BOBBIE** *tries to stop* **JOHN**.)*

Sir!

*(***JOHN** *rushes into* **ELEANOR**'s *office.)*

ELEANOR. Excuse me?!

JOHN. What the hell…?

ELEANOR. How dare you storm into my…?

JOHN. *(Holding up letter.)* You can't do this.

ELEANOR. *(Calmly.)* No?

JOHN. This isn't legal.

ELEANOR. Sure it is.

JOHN. This is my company.

ELEANOR. Not anymore.

JOHN. You had no right. Marley assured me that he would never…

ELEANOR. Marley's history.

JOHN. Doesn't matter. He promised…

ELEANOR. *(Rises and snatches the memo from* **JOHN.***)* Jacob Marley was a business man, Misslehouse. This is business. He would have done the same thing. You put shares up for sale and I bought them.

JOHN. But…

ELEANOR. You play with fire, you're going to get burned.

JOHN. Now, see here, I…

ELEANOR. People can be divided into three groups, Misslehouse. Those who make things happen. Those who watch things happen. And those who wonder what happened. Which do you think you are?

JOHN. Well…

ELEANOR. *(***ELEANOR** *signs the memo and hands it back to* **JOHN.***)*
Enjoy the view.

JOHN. My gramps built this company from the ground up. He gave his life to make it happen. Started from a cabin with a tin roof.

*(***ELEANOR** *pretends like she is interested.)*

In Kalamazoo. Had the water pumped up from a fresh water creek. I'll never forget, on my eighteenth birthday, my pop handed me keys, put his arm around me and said..

ELEANOR. Blah. Blahbitty. Blah. Save it for Hallmark. I have things to do.

JOHN. You've stolen my name.

ELEANOR. I'm changing the name. It's dull and uninspired.

JOHN. How dare you…?

ELEANOR. And I didn't steal it. I bought it. Now if you'll excuse me.

(**ELEANOR** *goes back to her computer.*)

JOHN. I'll fight you. All the way to the supreme court if I have to.

ELEANOR. That could be expensive. Better have Gramps build another shack.

JOHN. (*Shaking his head in disbelief.*) Everything they said about you is true.

ELEANOR. "They" are jealous. Amateurs. Like you, Mistletoe.

JOHN. This is only the beginning. You will get the justice you deserve.

ELEANOR. Such drama.

JOHN. You haven't heard the last of me.

ELEANOR. Oh, goodie.

(**JOHN** *rushes for the door, passing* **BOBBIE**. **JOHN** *crashes into* **PHIL,** *who enters the office.* **JOHN** *tries to pull himself together but is on the verge of a panic attack. He stumbles out.*)

JOHN. Sorry.

PHIL. That's alright. You okay?

(**ELEANOR** *watches* **JOHN** *out, calling to him as he exits.*)

ELEANOR. Happy holidays!

(**ELEANOR** *laughs devilishly. Her smiles abruptly disappears when she sees* **PHIL**. **PHIL** *holds a Christmas tin of cookies with a bow on top.*)

ELEANOR. Phillip? What are you doing here?

PHIL. Hey, Aunt Eleanor.

> (**ELEANOR** *frowns. She hates being called "Aunt."* **PHIL**
> *walks up to her and kisses her on the cheek.* **ELEANOR**
> *squirms.*)

PHIL. How are you?

ELEANOR. Busy. What do you want?

PHIL. I wanted to invite you over tomorrow. For Christmas
dinner.

ELEANOR. I'm working.

> (*To* **BOBBIE.**)

> Some people are more dedicated to this company than
> others.

> (**ELEANOR** *re-enters her office.* **PHIL** *follows.*)

PHIL. On Christmas?

ELEANOR. It's a Thursday, Phillip.

PHIL. So take off early. Carla bought a huge turkey. It will
take hours to…

ELEANOR. Thank you, but I have to finish a proposal.

> (**ELEANOR** *shouts out to* **BOBBIE.**)

> Because I have to do it myself, it will take all day and
> likely half the night.

PHIL. Well, what about tonight? For drinks. We're having a
few people…

> (**ELEANOR** *begins to close her door.*)

> You haven't seen Carla since the wedding. She made
> her special cookies, just for you.

> (*He puts the Christmas tin on her desk.*)

ELEANOR. Some other time.

PHIL. How's Sunday?

ELEANOR. Check my calendar.

> (**ELEANOR** *gestures to* **BOBBIE.**)

PHIL. Okay. Well, Merry…

> (**ELEANOR** *closes her door. To himself.*)

…Christmas.

BOBBIE. Merry Christmas, Phil.

(**PHIL** *smiles at* **BOBBIE** *and crosses to her desk.* **ELEANOR** *opens the tin and holds up a cookie. It is burned.*)

PHIL. How's it going, Bobbie?

BOBBIE. Good. Thanks.

PHIL. Why don't you join us tomorrow? I'm telling you this turkey is huge…What do you say?

BOBBIE. Thanks. That's very sweet, but…well…Tim…he… it's tough…with the snow.

PHIL. How is he?

BOBBIE. Great.

(**BOBBIE** *smiles awkwardly. She looks down.* **ELEANOR** *throws* **PHIL***'s cookie tin in the trash.*)

PHIL. Well, you're welcome anytime. Consider it an open invite.

BOBBIE. Let's check that schedule, huh?

(**BOBBIE** *opens the appointment calendar.* **ELEANOR** *picks up the receiver and dials.* **BOBBIE***'s intercom phone rings. To* **PHIL***:*)

BOBBIE. Excuse me.

(**BOBBIE** *picks up the receiver.* **PHIL** *unwraps a Christmas chocolate "kiss" from a bowl on* **BOBBIE***'s desk and pops it in his mouth.*)

ELEANOR. Get rid of him.

(**BOBBIE** *picks up the receiver.*)

BOBBIE. But, Ma'am, are you sure you don't…?

ELEANOR. What have I taught you about loyalty?

BOBBIE. Ma'am?

ELEANOR. Loyalty, Cratchit.

BOBBIE. Uh…a dog will never bite the hand that leads it?

ELEANOR. No.

BOBBIE. That needs it?

ELEANOR. Wrong.

BOBBIE. That heeds it?

(**ELEANOR** *makes a buzzer sound.*)

I'm sorry, Ma'am. I'm afraid I don't quite remember that one.

ELEANOR. Should I print you out another copy of the list?

BOBBIE. Yes…No! It won't happen again.

(**ELEANOR** *hangs up on* **BOBBIE**. **BOBBIE** *looks at* **PHIL**, *still holding the receiver.*)

Oh…Of course, glad I could be of help…No, thank you.

(*Bobbie hangs up the phone.*)

PHIL. So, how's Sunday for the ole battle ax?

BOBBIE. Booked.

PHIL. Friday?

BOBBIE. Booked.

PHIL. Saturday?

BOBBIE. No.

PHIL. Next Sunday?

(**BOBBIE** *shakes her head "no."* **ELEANOR** *turns her intercom button on, stands, and listens in on the conversation between* **BOBBIE** *and* **PHIL**.)

Next week?

(**BOBBIE** *shakes her head "no."*)

That was her, wasn't it? Telling you to give me the 'ole heave Ho Ho Ho.

(**BOBBIE** *looks down again.*)

PHIL. It's alright. I'm getting used to it.

(**PHIL** *crosses to the thermostat.*)

It's freezing in here. The heat busted?

(**PHIL** *reaches his hand toward the thermostat.*)

BOBBIE. NO! It's…she likes it cold.

(**BOBBIE** *runs over to* **PHIL** *to stop him.*)

PHIL. God bless you. I don't know how you do it.

BOBBIE. She has…some good traits.

PHIL. Yeah? Tell me one, would you? So I can let my wife know…just one.

BOBBIE. She's…She's uh…

PHIL. I'm listening.

BOBBIE. She's…She's very…

(**PHIL** *laughs and crosses to* **BOBBIE**. *He kisses her on the cheek.*)

PHIL. I'll see ya.

(**BOBBIE** *nods.* **PHIL** *crosses to the door.*)

Tell Snow Miser Merry Christmas for me. And give Timmy my best.

BOBBIE. I will.

(**ELEANOR** *switches off the intercom button, angrily.*)

PHIL. Bobbie, if you ever need anything, anything at all, don't hesitate…

BOBBIE. Thanks.

PHIL. I could take him to a Giants game! Anytime he wants. My boss has great seats. Smack down on the fifty yard line…

(**ELEANOR** *dials the phone. It rings on* **BOBBIE**'s *desk.*)

Right.

(**PHIL** *smiles and exits.* **BOBBIE** *slowly picks up the receiver.*)

ELEANOR. My office. Now.

(**ELEANOR** *slams down the receiver.* **BOBBIE** *lowers the receiver and slowly crosses into* **ELEANOR**'s *office.*)

ELEANOR. Do you enjoy working here, Cratchit?

BOBBIE. Yes, Ma'am. Of course.

ELEANOR. Why?

BOBBIE. Ma'am?

ELEANOR. You do realize I have invested a great deal of time and resources into making you what you are today? Wisdom does not come cheap.

BOBBIE. Yes, Ma'am...no, Ma'am. I'm...honored.

ELEANOR. People would kill for this kind of education... dedication.

BOBBIE. I'm sure. I'm very thankful, Ma'am. To have you as my boss...my mentor.

ELEANOR. Are you?

BOBBIE. Ma'am?

ELEANOR. Thankful. To be saddled with a...a...snow miser?

BOBBIE. *(Realizing* **ELEANOR** *was eavesdropping)* No, Ma'am... You are not...you are...you...

ELEANOR. Yes?

BOBBIE. You are...such a hard worker.

ELEANOR. Uh-huh.

BOBBIE. And a master of motivational speaking.

ELEANOR. Go on.

BOBBIE. A dynamic business woman.

(**ELEANOR** *laughs.*)

ELEANOR. True.

BOBBIE. The Queen of Wall Street.

ELEANOR. Queen. I like that.

BOBBIE. You're a financial wizard.

ELEANOR. Well.

BOBBIE. A genius, really.

(**ELEANOR** *nods)*

And when they invite you to ring the opening bell... which they will very soon...I will be there...cheering you on...wishing you everything that you deserve.

(**ELEANOR** *looks at* **BOBBIE.** **BOBBIE** *quickly rebounds.)*

You put the Dow in Jones, the stock in market, the must in buy. You are the most evil-tempered woman I have ever known.

(ELEANOR glares at BOBBIE.)

Even. Even-tempered.

(BOBBIE turns to leave and crashes into ELEANOR's desk, sending her cup of pens flying. BOBBIE crawls on the floor and picks up the pens. She reaches up and feels around for the pen cup. She mistakenly grabs ELEANOR's take-out coffee cup, rises, puts the pens in the cup and hands the cup to ELEANOR. ELEANOR slowly takes it and pulls the pens out as BOBBIE watches. Coffee drips from the bottom of the pens. Petrified, BOBBIE smiles awkwardly.)

ELEANOR. Lock the door!

(BOBBIE runs out of ELEANOR's office and crosses to the door. She begins to close it when SARAH and BEN enter, with a Christmas boot they use to collect donations. ELEANOR exits into her bathroom with the pens.)

SARAH/BEN. Happy Holidays!

BOBBIE. *(Quietly.)* Happy Holidays.

SARAH. Is this the office of Marley, Scrooge and Associates?

BOBBIE. Scrooge, Inc. and…

(Bobbie holds up her hand.)

Associate.

BEN. Is Mr. Scrooge or Mr. Marley available?

BOBBIE. Mr. Marley recently…passed on. And Ms. Scrooge is not…

SARAH. My name is Sarah. And this is Ben.

(BEN nods, smiles.)

BEN. We're volunteers for the Manhattan Coalition for Humanity.

(BOBBIE enters from her bathroom, wiping the pens off with a paper towel. She puts the pens back in the proper

cup. She grabs the coffee cup and heads to the trash can to throw it out.)

SARAH/BEN. Homeless helpers!

BEN. At this time of year…

SARAH. With temperatures hovering around the freezing point…

BEN. The homeless population is facing a daily struggle for survival.

ELEANOR. *(Hearing something. Into intercom.)* Cratchit?

(**BOBBIE** *tries to get back to her desk, but* **SARAH** *and* **BEN** *block her path.)*

SARAH. It is up to our citizens…

BOBBIE. *(Trying to get to her intercom.)* …excuse me…

BEN. The leaders of our fair city…

ELEANOR. Cratchit, are you there?

SARAH. To ensure that these unfortunate souls have the support they need to…

BOBBIE. I really have to…

ELEANOR. *(Flinging open her office door.)* Cratchit!

(**SARAH** *and* **BEN** *abruptly stop talking.)*

SARAH. Is that Ms. Scrooge?

(**BOBBIE** *nods "yes."* **SARAH** *and* **BEN** *quickly cross to Eleanor.)*

SARAH/BEN. Happy Holidays!

ELEANOR. Cratchit?

SARAH. My name is Sarah. And this is Ben.

(**BEN** *nods, smiles)*

BEN. We're volunteers for the Manhattan Coalition for Humanity.

SARAH/BEN. Homeless helpers!

BEN. At this time of year…

SARAH. With temperatures hovering around the freezing point…

BEN. The homeless population is facing a daily struggle for survival.

ELEANOR. Get out.

SARAH. It is up to our citizens…

BEN. The leaders of our fair city…

ELEANOR. Out!

SARAH. But…Ms. Scrooge, we need you.

BEN. Your donation will go toward helping the HHF…

SARAH. Homeless Helper Foundation.

BEN. …build a permanent center for the homeless.

SARAH. Right here in Manhattan.

BEN. To provide a shelter.

SARAH. A warm place.

BEN. A safe place.

SARAH/BEN. To sleep.

ELEANOR. Subways are warm.

SARAH. It's Christmas.

ELEANOR. Represented by a demented fat man in velvet. If Cringle was my client, I would advise him to ditch the elves, eat the deer, and have his toys made in China.

(**BEN** and **SARAH** look stunned.)

So.

(To **SARAH**)

Go.

(To **BEN**)

So I can work.

(To **SARAH**)

And forget.

(To **BEN**)

That you.

(To **SARAH**)

Ever.

(*To* **BEN**)

Were here.

(**SARAH** *smiles and holds out the Christmas boot for a donation.* **ELEANOR** *pours the contents of her take-out coffee into the boot.* **SARAH** *begins to cry.*)

Oh, for god's sake. Cratchit, call security.

(**ELEANOR** *exits into her office, slamming the door behind her.* **BEN** *leads* **SARAH** *to the door.*)

BOBBIE. Hold on.

(**BOBBIE** *grabs her change purse and fishes through it for some change but it is empty. She slowly unwraps her scarf from her neck and hands it to* **BEN**.)

It's not much, but take it. Please.

(**BEN** *takes the scarf.*)

BEN. Bless you.

(**BEN** *smiles at* **BOBBIE** *and exits with* **SARAH**. **BOBBIE** *locks the door. She crosses back to her chair and sits, shivering.*)

ELEANOR. *(Into intercom.)* Is the door locked?

BOBBIE. *(Into intercom.)* Yes, Ma'am.

ELEANOR. *(Into intercom.)* This is not the Red Cross, Cratchit. It's bad enough there are beggars, now there are beggars' beggars? You should know better. God only knows where that boot has been. Charities are the scourge of modern civilization.

BOBBIE. *(Into intercom.)* Yes, Ma'am.

(*A beat.*)

ELEANOR. *(Into intercom.)* I suppose you want the whole day off tomorrow?

BOBBIE. *(Into intercom.)* If at all possible.

ELEANOR. *(Into intercom.)* The deadline for the Newman merger is firm, Cratchit. If we lose the deal, I may have to downsize.

BOBBIE. *(Into intercom.)* I'll get here early on Friday.

ELEANOR. *(Into intercom.)* Good.

BOBBIE. *(Into intercom.)* 7:30?

ELEANOR. *(Into intercom.)* 7:00.

BOBBIE. (**BOBBIE** *picks up a framed picture of* **TIMMY**. *Into intercom.)* Ma'am?

ELEANOR. *(Into intercom.)* What?

BOBBIE. *(Into intercom.)* Well…about my health insurance. The HMO won't cover a procedure that Tim's doctor is recommending. It's very expensive. I think it could really help him to…

ELEANOR. *(Into intercom.)* You want a raise.

BOBBIE. *(Into intercom.)* Or an upgrade in coverage. I would greatly appreciate it, ma'am. It could make all the…

ELEANOR. *(Into intercom.)* This is not a good time, Bobbie.

BOBBIE. An advance against my future earnings?

ELEANOR. The market could take a bad turn at any time. It's very volatile. You know that as well as anyone. She who gets fat on the feast suffers most in the famine.

BOBBIE. Yes, Ma'am.

(A beat. **BOBBIE** *wants to respond but thinks better of it. She packs her briefcase again.)*

ELEANOR. *(Into intercom.)* I'll see you at 7 a.m. on Friday… Sharp.

BOBBIE. *(Into intercom.)* Good night.

ELEANOR. *(Into intercom)* Turn out the reception lights.

BOBBIE. *(Into intercom.)* Shall I wait to walk you out?

ELEANOR. *(Into intercom, with her feet up on the desk, flipping through a Forbes magazine.)*
I'm working, Roberta. I have way too much to do to leave. Especially now that you're deserting me.

*(***BOBBIE*** *finishes packing up and struggles to carry the overstuffed briefcase to the door.)*

Turn the thermostat back down.

(**BOBBIE** *crosses to the door. She turns out the lights in her area. The lights stay on in* **ELEANOR**'s *office.* **BOBBIE** *considers. She crosses back to the intercom.*)

BOBBIE. *(With a devilish grin. Into intercom.)* Merry Christmas, Eleanor!

ELEANOR. *(Rises quickly. Into intercom.)* Double-lock the doors!

(**BOBBIE** *exits, double-locking the doors with her keys from outside the door.* **ELEANOR** *picks up her phone and dials an extension.*)

Hello? Where's Sanders?…Of course. Who are you? Sven? Well, Sven, this is…right. Don't let anyone up to the 16th floor. I'm working late…I'll be fine…Yes… Whatever.

(**ELEANOR**'s *phone rings. She picks it up.*)

ELEANOR. Hello?

(There is no response. She hangs up the phone. The phone rings in **BOBBIE**'s *office.* **ELEANOR** *crosses to the door. She turns on the light and crosses to* **BOBBIE**'s *desk. She picks up the phone)*

ELEANOR. Hello?!

(There is no response. **ELEANOR** *hangs up the phone. She crosses back to her door and turns off the light to* **BOBBIE**'s *area. The front door buzzer goes off.* **ELEANOR** *turns the light back on. There is no one there. A beat.* **ELEANOR** *turns the light off. She re-enters her office and closes the door. The sound of loud stock market bells.* **ELEANOR** *jumps in fright.* **ELEANOR** *rings the small miniature bell on her desk (a completely different sound/ tone) She slowly sits at her desk and picks up the phone receiver. She dials the front desk on level 1.)*

ELEANOR. Sven?…Where's Sven?…I just spoke with him… Are you leaving, too?…Good. Is there something wrong with the phones?…The power?…Nevermind!

(ELEANOR hangs up the phone. She starts working on her computer. There is a tapping on the window behind her. ELEANOR slowly crosses to the window. Tapping continues. ELEANOR opens the blinds. MARLEY appears. He smiles and waves at ELEANOR, who screams and leaps back. She quickly lowers the blinds. A beat. ELEANOR slowly raises the blinds. MARLEY is gone. ELEANOR moves close to the window and looks out. She slowly lowers the blinds and flops down into her chair. She picks up the phone and dials an extension.)

I need a triple expresso with a double shot on the 16th floor…Eleanor Scrooge…What do you mean you can't leave the desk?…Well, then, send somebody up…How can you be the only security person left? There's fifty floors in this building…I know what night it is!

(ELEANOR slams down the phone. She goes back to her computer, mumbling to herself. MARLEY comes through the wall in ELEANOR's office and leans over her, watching her work on the computer.)

MARLEY. Don't hold. Sell. Dump it all.

(ELEANOR slowly turns around and looks at MARLEY. She screams. MARLEY jumps back, holding his ears. ELEANOR backs away from the desk.)

Oww! For god's sake, El.

ELEANOR. Jacob?

MARLEY. *(Looking around)* What did you do with my Queen Ann Desk?

(He taps on her desk.)

This isn't even real wood.

ELEANOR. What are you doing here?

MARLEY. No "how's it going"? "I missed you"? "Hostile takeovers aren't nearly as much fun since you left?"

ELEANOR. I'm dreaming. This is a nightmare.

MARLEY. A nightmare? So now I'm a nightmare? That's gratitude.

ELEANOR. This isn't happening.

MARLEY. Oh, it's happening. At least you kept my chair.

(MARLEY *sits in the desk chair and stares at the computer.*)

Why are you buying more of this stock? It's going to go bust after New Year's.

ELEANOR. Really?

MARLEY. Completely bankrupt. Will make Enron look like a must-buy.

ELEANOR. (*No longer afraid.*) You're kidding?

MARLEY. (*Shakes his head.*) Consider it insider information.

ELEANOR. How…how do you know?

MARLEY. I know all kinds of new things, El. They keep us very up to speed on current events.

ELEANOR. Are you…an angel?

MARLEY. No such luck.

(*He bows his head and leans into* ELEANOR.)

See 'em?

ELEANOR. See what?

MARLEY. Feel around…go ahead.

(ELEANOR *slowly runs her fingers over* MARLEY*'s head.* ELEANOR *feels his horns, gasps, quickly pulls her hand away.*)

Nice, huh? They're just starting to come in. Takes a while.

(MARLEY *scratches his head.*)

Except they've been itching me like crazy lately.

(ELEANOR *is mortified.*)

ELEANOR. Am I…dead, Marley?

MARLEY. No. At least not in the traditional sense. But I got to tell you, there's not much holding your soul into place.

ELEANOR. Are you here to take me…down?

MARLEY. I can't. I don't have that clout. And you don't want to go, trust me. I'm low man on the totem pole. Have to spend eternity as an intern.

*(*ELEANOR *gasps.)*

Making coffee, emptying trash, licking envelopes. And the boss hates me. I can't do anything right. They'll send somebody else. With a diversified portfolio and a slew of dedicated clients.

(He touches his head.)

And bigger horns.

ELEANOR. But I don't want to be an intern. Not again.

MARLEY. It's not up to me, Kid. Tell it to your advisors.

ELEANOR. Advisors?

MARLEY. Spirits. Three of them. They'll be stopping by later.

*(*MARLEY *smiles.)*

To haunt you.

*(*MARLEY *walks into* BOBBIE*'s area and snaps his finger, lighting up the area.)*

My god, Eleanor, where'd you get this crap? The salvation army?

(He sees the "And Marley" crossed out on the front door.)

Oh, nice. Real nice.

ELEANOR. *(Following him.)* What am I supposed to do?

MARLEY. You got one chance to seal the deal, Eleanor. Remember the golden be's?

ELEANOR. Be cool. Be calm. Be…Be…Be…

MARLEY. Be quiet! Listen for a change. Don't blow it like you did that Wordsworth Consortium deal.

ELEANOR. I did not blow it, Jacob. That deal was dead before I even sat at the table. You can lead a horse to water but you can't make him drink. He who hesitates is lost. It's not the size of the dog in the fight, it's the size of the fight in…

MARLEY. Don't! Stop it, right now! Save the Scroogisms for your clients. I can't take it.

ELEANOR. I thought you liked them?

MARLEY. You pull out one those tonight and you're toast. You understand?

ELEANOR. Jacob. You mean to tell me all those years…

MARLEY. Shhh. I said to listen, Eleanor.

(*Shakes his head.*)

Gotta go.

ELEANOR. Wait! Who…what…when…where…?

MARLEY. You got about a minute. Use it wisely.

ELEANOR. What should I do?

MARLEY. You pray?

ELEANOR. What??

MARLEY. Call someone you love.

(**ELEANOR** *gives him a blank look.*)

Relative?

(**ELEANOR** *gives him another look.*)

Friend?

(**ELEANOR** *glares at him.*)

Right. Let's have a drink.

(*He quickly begins opening and closing drawers.*)

Where's my bottle of Royal Salute?

(**ELEANOR** *shrugs sheepishly.*)

You hocked it, didn't you? With my furniture.

ELEANOR. (*Lying*) Of course not.

MARLEY. Okay, Kid. The odds don't look good.

(*Patting her on the arm.*)

But do your best.

(**MARLEY** *starts for the closet.*)

ELEANOR. Jacob, I'm afraid.

MARLEY. You? Afraid? Come on.

(**MARLEY** *crosses to the closet.*)

ELEANOR. Hold on. What's your angle?

MARLEY. Angle? I'm just looking out for your best interests.

(**ELEANOR** *doesn't buy it.* **MARLEY** *smiles and holds open his arms.*)

I've missed you, Kid.

(**ELEANOR** *glares at* **MARLEY**. **MARLEY** *drops the ruse.*)

Alright, it's like this…if you can change your destiny, I have a chance to be re-assigned. Otherwise, there's eight million more boxes of envelopes with my name on them. So, please, be on your game today? No words of wisdom, for god's sake. And sell that stock. It's crap.

(**ELEANOR** *rushes to her computer.* **MARLEY** *opens the closet door and takes a final look.*)

God, I miss the cold.

(**MARLEY** *exits into the closet.*)

ELEANOR. Jacob?

(**ELEANOR** *rushes to the closet door and flings it open. There is no one inside.*)

Jacob?

(**ELEANOR** *backs away. She sits in her chair, rubbing her eyes. She looks around.*)

Hello? Anyone there?

(*No response.*)

Spirits. Ha!

(*She begins typing frantically [she's selling, just in case]. There is a buzzer at the front door to the reception area.* **ELEANOR** *cowers in her chair. There is another buzzer [longer].* **ELEANOR** *slowly opens the door to her office and turns the light on to the reception area.* **ELEANOR**

sees a young man through the glass door. She breathes
a sigh of relief and crosses to the door, unlocking both
locks. She opens the door.)

ELEANOR. Well?

PAST. Excuse me?

ELEANOR. Where is it?

(**PAST** *looks blankly at* **ELEANOR.**)

My expresso!

(**PAST** *looks blankly at* **ELEANOR.**)

Oh, I can see as per usual they get only the really bright
ones to work the holidays.

PAST. You got to be Eleanor Scrooge.

ELEANOR. *(Steps back)* How dare you address me by my first
name? You grunts on the night shift think you can get
away with anything.

(**PAST** *walks into the office. He looks around.*)

ELEANOR. What is the name of your supervisor?

PAST. You don't know him.

ELEANOR. I will by tomorrow morning, I assure you. And
you'll be out of a job.

(**PAST** *laughs.* **ELEANOR** *is appalled.*)

Get out.

(**ELEANOR** *crosses to the door and opens it.*)

I said to get out.

PAST. You're wasting valuable time, Eleanor.

ELEANOR. Now!

(**PAST** *smiles and walks out.* **ELEANOR** *shuts the door*
and double-locks it.)

PAST. You can't keep me away.

ELEANOR. No? No one has a key to that top lock but me
and my assistant.

(**ELEANOR** *storms back to her office door. She turns and* *looks at* **PAST**, *who is still standing at the glass door.)*

You're fired.

*(***ELEANOR*** *smiles.)*

Happy Holidays!

*(***ELEANOR*** *shuts off the light to the reception area. She enters her office and locks the door. She sits at her desk and picks up the phone. She dials a number from her Rolodex.)*

John Westbrook, please…Well, wake him up…I know what night it is!

*(***PAST*** *walks through the wall just upstage of the glass door and walks through the darkness towards* **ELEA-NOR**'s *office.* **ELEANOR** *swivels her chair as she talks on the phone so that she is looking out the window. She does not see* **PAST** *walk through the wall, upstage of her door.)*

ELEANOR. Tell him it's Ms. Scrooge from the 16th floor. That will get him out of bed. Scrooge. S-C-R-double O-G-E…Listen, Sweetie: either wake him up or let him sleep all week 'cause he won't have a job to go to… Thank you.

*(***PAST*** *sits in a chair and watches* **ELEANOR**.*)*

Westbrook. It's Scrooge…Yeah, well, it *is* an emergency. One of your rejects just verbally assaulted me…Yes. I think it's Ben…or Len…or Ken. He's Oriental.

PAST. Asian.

ELEANOR. About 5'10."

PAST. 6'.

ELEANOR. 6'. I don't know. Maybe twenty-four, twenty-five.

PAST. Five hundred and eighty two.

ELEANOR. Five hundred and…

(It sinks in. **ELEANOR** *looks at* **PAST**. *He waves.* **ELEA-NOR** *dives under the desk.)*

PAST. *(In* **ELEANOR**'s *voice)* Westbrook?…No, false alarm. I guess I shouldn't mix my medications. It's just there's *sooo* many to manage.

(**ELEANOR** *peaks her head up and gasps.*)

Sorry to disturb you…Why don't you order watches for you and your men…from Cartier…any style you want. Charge it to my account…Yes, see you Tuesday. Unless I check myself into Betty Ford. Aloha!

(**PAST** *hangs up the receiver.*)

ELEANOR. Are you…my advisor?

PAST. More of a guide.

ELEANOR. Your name isn't Ken, is it?

PAST. *(Shakes his head.)* Past.

ELEANOR. Pest?

PAST. Past! Your past, Eleanor. Or should I call you Ellie?

ELEANOR. *(Slowly rises.)* No one has called me that in…

PAST. Twenty years?

ELEANOR. *(Shocked.)* How did you…?

(**PAST** *walks through the wall. He sticks his head back into the office.*)

PAST. Come on.

(**ELEANOR** *hesitates.*)

Let's go.

(**ELEANOR** *comes through the door and joins* **PAST** *in the area downstage of the office.* **PAST** *snaps his fingers and the lights come up on the area [different lights than before] and out on* **ELEANOR**'s *office.* **ROBERT** *stands holding a Christmas tree. He checks his watch.*)

ELEANOR. Robert!

(**ELEANOR** *rushes to* **ROBERT**. **ROBERT** *does not react to her.*)

Robert? He can't hear me.

PAST. You think?

(*Tug, a vendor enters.*)

TUG. We're closing up. You want the tree or not?

ROBERT. Just a few more minutes, please. I promised my girlfriend we'd pick it out together.

TUG. You got five.

*(Tug walks off. **ROBERT** looks at his watch again. He holds up the tree and smiles. **ELLIE** rushes in.)*

ELLIE. Robert?

*(**ROBERT** turns and sees **ELLIE**. She rushes into his arms and they embrace.)*

ELEANOR. That's…

PAST/ELEANOR. You./Me.

ELLIE. Sorry I'm late. Mr. Marley needed a report that couldn't wait. A merger. It would mean big things for the company, Robert. Great things.

ROBERT. It's okay.

(He holds up the tree.)

You like it?

ELLIE. I do. Very much. Let's take it home and decorate it.

ROBERT. Now? It's ten o'clock.

ELLIE. I don't care. I love Christmas, Robert.

ROBERT. I love you.

(They kiss.)

ELLIE. Come on.

(They start off with the tree.)

ROBERT. *(Laughs)* Wait. I have to pay for it.

ELLIE. Let's make a run for it.

ROBERT. What? Ellie.

ELLIE. Chicken.

ROBERT. You're bad.

ELLIE. *(Smiles)* You have no idea.

ROBERT. I have a surprise for you.

ELLIE. What is it?

ROBERT. You have to wait until Christmas.

*(***ELLIE*** *tickles* ***ROBERT.****)*

ELLIE. What is it?

*(***ROBERT*** *pulls away [he's very ticklish].)*

ROBERT. You have to wait, Ellie.

ELLIE. But I don't want to.

ROBERT. It's only a week.

*(***TUG*** *enters.)*

TUG. The girlfriend?

ROBERT. Yes.

TUG. So?

ROBERT. We'll take it.

TUG. Terrific.

*(***ROBERT*** *hands* ***TUG*** *a few bills.)*

ELLIE. It's a beautiful tree.

TUG. Gorgeous.

*(***TUG*** *starts off.)*

ELLIE. Wait.

*(***TUG*** *stops and looks at* ***ELLIE*** *impatiently.* ***ELLIE*** *takes a small candy cane from her purse and hands it to* ***TUG.****)*

Merry Christmas.

*(***TUG*** *looks at* ***ELLIE*** *as if she is insane.* ***ELLIE*** *takes* ***ROBERT*** *by the hand and they joyfully exit with the tree.* ***TUG*** *exits via the opposite side of stage.)*

ELEANOR. Can I talk to him?

PAST. Nope.

ELEANOR. Just for a minute?

PAST. 'Fraid not.

ELEANOR. Please.

PAST. Why? What would you say? Absence makes the heart grow fonder?

ELEANOR. I don't talk like that.

PAST. Oh, no? Marley was right. You're like a bad fortune cookie.

ELEANOR. What is the point of this? I have work to do.

PAST. Listen.

(PAST *snaps his fingers again. The lights shift on the same area.* TESS *is wheeled in by a nurse.*)

TESS. By the window, please.

(*The nurse wheels* TESS *to an area where a window light spills through.*)

Thank you.

(*The nurse exits.* ELEANOR *rushes to* TESS. *She kneels by the wheelchair.*)

ELEANOR. Tess? Tess?

PAST. She can't hear you.

ELEANOR. Oh, Tess. I've missed you. I've missed you so much.

(ELEANOR *hugs* TESS. TESS *does not react, continuing to look out the window.* ELEANOR *slowly releases her and backs away.* YOUNG PHIL *rushes in.*)

YOUNG PHIL. Look, Mama.

(*He hands* TESS *a Christmas card.*)

ELEANOR. Phillip?

YOUNG PHIL. I made this. For Aunt Ellie.

(PAST *crosses to* ELEANOR *and gently pulls her away.*)

TESS. Oh, honey. It's beautiful.

YOUNG PHIL. The nurse helped me a little.

TESS. It's the best Christmas card I've ever seen.

YOUNG PHIL. You think Aunt Ellie will like it?

TESS. She'll love it.

YOUNG PHIL. Where is she going to take me?

TESS. I don't know. Somewhere fun, I'm sure.

YOUNG PHIL. Can we go sledding?

TESS. Maybe. You'll have to ask her.

(**YOUNG PHIL** *hugs* **TESS.**)

YOUNG PHIL. I wish you could go.

TESS. I know, sweetheart.

(*Overwhelmed,* **ELEANOR** *starts back toward her office.*)

PAST. You can't run away from your past, Eleanor. You have to face it.

(**ELEANOR** *turns and rejoins Past.*)

YOUNG PHIL. Should I wrap it?

TESS. Sure. Get Nurse Laura to help you, okay?

YOUNG PHIL. Okay!

(**YOUNG PHIL** *rushes off happily.* **TESS** *looks out the window.* **ELLIE** *enters.*)

ELLIE. Sorry. The office is insane. We just got a lead on…

TESS. You scared me. I didn't think you were coming.

ELLIE. Why? I know I'm a little late, but…

TESS. Phillip is really looking forward to this.

ELLIE. Hey, guess what? I found a great new doctor I want you to see. He's out of Boston.

TESS. Ellie.

ELLIE. He is supposed to be the best. Jacob says he's at the forefront of…

TESS. I have a doctor.

ELLIE. Not like this one.

TESS. I trust him.

ELLIE. Yeah, well, be leery of loyalty and suspicious of sincerity.

(**PAST** *sighs, shaking his head.*)

TESS. Stop it…

ELLIE. At least let me schedule an appointment.

TESS. Listen to me.

ELLIE. What do you have to…

TESS. Listen to me! Please…Mom wants to adopt Phillip.

ELLIE. Adopt him? Why?

TESS. Ellie. It's time.

> (**TESS** *takes* **ELLIE**'s *hand.*)

I want him to be with you. And Robert.

ELLIE. I don't understand.

TESS. He'd be an excellent father, Ellie.

> (**ELLIE** *gently pulls away.*)

Mom's too old to be raising children.

ELLIE. What would it hurt to meet with Doctor Henry? Just meet with him, please.

> (**MARLEY** *enters, sporting a mustache.*)

MARLEY. El?

> (**ELEANOR** *turns to* **MARLEY**. **MARLEY** *points to his watch.*)

ELEANOR. Go away!

TESS. What is he…?

> (**YOUNG PHIL** *rushes in.*)

YOUNG PHIL. Aunt Ellie!

> (**YOUNG PHIL** *rushes into* **ELLIE**'s *arms.*)

ELLIE. Hi! How's my favorite nephew?

YOUNG PHIL. (*Laughing.*) I'm your only nephew, silly.

ELLIE. Well, you're worth two nephews. At least.

YOUNG PHIL. I made something for you.

> (**YOUNG PHIL** *presents* **ELLIE** *with the wrapped card.*)

ELLIE. Thank you.

MARLEY. Eleanor. We're going to be late.

> (**ELLIE** *rises and puts the card in her purse without looking at it.*)

YOUNG PHIL. Can we go sledding today?

ELLIE. Well, I'm not really dressed for sledding. Maybe next time, okay?

YOUNG PHIL. So, what are we going to do?

ELLIE. Well…Actually, I have a meeting I have to got to for a few hours. But…I'll be back by six.

MARLEY. Seven.

ELLIE. Seven at the latest.

(Phil looks at **TESS.***)*

I promise…

*(***ELLIE*** looks at* **TESS.***)*

I promise.

*(***TESS*** looks away.)*

I'll tell you what. I'll take you to the mall, okay, and we'll buy you any present you want.

YOUNG PHIL. Really? Any one I want?

MARLEY. For god's sake. Give the kid a twenty and let's go.

ELLIE. Any one you want.

*(***ELLIE*** kisses* **YOUNG PHIL** *on the cheek. She reaches over to kiss* **TESS,** *but* **TESS** *pulls her head away.)*

I'll see you later, okay?

YOUNG PHIL. Okay.

ELLIE. Here.

(She hands **TESS** *a business card.)*

It's Doctor Henry's card. Call him, okay?

*(***ELLIE*** starts out. She turns back to* **TESS.***)*

I'll give you an answer when I get back. Okay?

TESS. I have my answer.

*(***ELLIE*** looks at* **TESS** *for a moment and then exits with* **MARLEY.***)*

YOUNG PHIL. Where'd she go?

TESS. Get my coat.

(She struggles to get out of the wheelchair.)

ELEANOR. No! Don't go.

YOUNG PHIL. Really?

TESS. Really. Take this with you.

(**YOUNG PHIL** *gets in front of the wheelchair.*)

Put it in the bedroom and shut the door.

(**YOUNG PHIL** *starts out.*)

Quietly, okay? Don't let Nurse Laura see you.

YOUNG PHIL. (*Whispers*) Okay.

(**YOUNG PHIL** *wheels off the chair.* **TESS** *looks off at where* **ELLIE** *exited.*)

PAST. Her guilt made it worse.

ELEANOR. Excuse me?

PAST. It wasn't death that frightened her. It was leaving Phillip. It filled her with terrible guilt. And the one person…the only person who could make that pain go away…

(**PAST** *looks at* **ELEANOR.**)

Refused.

(**YOUNG PHIL** *re-enters, bundled up, holding* **TESS**'s *coat.*)

TESS. Did Nurse Laura see you?

(**YOUNG PHIL** *smiles and shakes his head.* **TESS** *smiles and ruffles* **YOUNG PHIL**'s *hair.*)

Come on.

(**TESS** *takes* **YOUNG PHIL**'s *hand and leads him away.*)

ELEANOR. Stop her. Stop her!

(**ELEANOR** *looks off to the direction* **TESS** *exited.*)

PAST. Don't you want to see what happened?

ELEANOR. No. Please. I'm begging you.

PAST. Turn around, Eleanor Scrooge.

ELEANOR. I loved her. I did. I never got to tell her how much.

PAST. Turn around. I haven't finished with you yet.

ELEANOR. Please. Don't show me anymore. I'll do anything.

PAST. Turn around!

> (**ELEANOR** *turns around.* **PAST** *snaps his fingers, and the lights shift in the same area.* **ROBERT** *is pacing.* **ELLIE** *rushes in and almost passes* **ROBERT**. *She doesn't notice him.*)

ROBERT. Ellie.

> (**ELLIE** *stops.*)

ELLIE. Robert? What are you doing here?

ROBERT. Waiting. For hours.

> (*Gestures to where she entered from.*)

Didn't your secretary tell you I was waiting outside?

ELLIE. I'm sorry. Between rushing back and forth from the office to the hospital, I've been crazy. I'm horribly behind on a contract.

ROBERT. You don't return my calls. You're never home.

ELLIE. My sister's dying, Robert.

> (**ROBERT** *crosses to* **ELLIE**.)

ROBERT. I want to be there for you. To help you through this.

ELLIE. I know...I...The timing is horrible. Jacob says if we get this contract through, he'll promote me. I'll be a full partner.

ROBERT. *(Flat)* That's great.

ELLIE. You're not happy for me?

ROBERT. I miss you, Ellie.

ELLIE. I know, but Oh, god, Robert. I can't do this now. I have to go.

> (**ROBERT** *takes* **ELLIE**'s *arm.*)

ROBERT. Wait. I never got a chance to give you your Christmas present.

> (*He takes a small package out of his coat pocket.*)

Open it.

ELLIE. Robert.

ROBERT. Please.

(**ELLIE** *snatches the present from* **ROBERT**. *She opens it quickly and then is stopped dead in her tracks when she realizes it is an engagement ring.*)

ROBERT. Before Tess collapsed, she called me.

(**ELLIE** *looks intently at* **ROBERT**.)

About Phillip. She…

(**ROBERT** *takes* **ELLIE***s hand.*)

She wanted to see if you'd take him. Adopt him. But she felt like she had to ask me first. She didn't want to do anything to break us up. She's a very special lady.

(**ELLIE** *pulls away.*)

Tess was going to talk to you about it. But then…Oh, honey. I just want to be with you. I love you. And I adore Phillip. I'd be happy to raise him. To be the father he never had. Let's start a family. Right now. I'm ready. I've never been so sure about anything in my life.

(**ROBERT** *kneels down and takes the ring. He begins to put it on* **ELLIE***'s finger when she backs away. She wells up.*)

ELLIE. I'm sorry.

(**ELLIE** *rushes off.* **ELEANOR** *crosses to* **ROBERT** *who stares at the ring.*)

ELEANOR. I loved him.

(*Looks at* **PAST**.)

I did.

PAST. Probably should have told him that.

ELEANOR. It wasn't the right time.

PAST. No?

(**ELEANOR** *crosses to* **ROBERT**.)

Funny thing about time. It's gone before you know it.

(**ROBERT** *walks off, leaving* **ELEANOR** *standing alone.*
PAST *snaps his fingers. The area goes black and the
lights come up on* **ELEANOR**'s *office (same as the lights
had been before the past was revealed).* **ELEANOR** *slowly
enters her office. She looks back into the dark reception
area. She quickly shuts her door and locks it. She wedges
a chair underneath the knob. She sits on the chair block-
ing the door, exhausted.* **PRESENT** *swings around in*
ELEANOR's *swivel chair behind the desk.*)

PRESENT. Whatcha doing?

(**ELEANOR** *sees the head in her desk and screams. She
runs into her private bathroom and slams the door
behind her.* **PRESENT** *appears from the desk. She is a
small woman, dressed in colorful Christmas garb. She
speaks with a Cockney accent.* **PRESENT** *calmly knocks
on the closet door.*)

You alright in there?

(**PRESENT** *knocks again.*)

ELEANOR. Go away. Please.

PRESENT. Sorry, love. No can do. Best come out so we can
chat a bit.

ELEANOR. And if I don't?

PRESENT. Oh, I don't know. I reckon I'll have to turn you
into a toad or lizard of some sort. Maybe a beetle. And
I don't mean George or Ringo.

ELEANOR. You wouldn't dare.

PRESENT. Or could be a combination of a slew of sorted
creatures. My spells are a bit off these days. Have a
mind of their own, I'm afraid.

(*The door slowly opens and* **ELEANOR** *slowly appears.*)

ELEANOR. Don't hurt me, please.

PRESENT. Do I look like I want to hurt you?

(**PRESENT** *screams suddenly at* **ELEANOR**, *causing*
ELEANOR *to scream.* **PRESENT** *laughs and gestures to
chair.*)

PRESENT. I've come to spend a bit of time, is all. Take a load off.

(**ELEANOR** *sits, petrified.*)

ELEANOR. Who are you?

PRESENT. I'm Present.

ELEANOR. Present?

PRESENT. Of time and space. Of here and now. See, with me, things are always what they seem. No room for reflection nor anticipation. What you see is what you get.

(**PRESENT** *smiles a big grin. She is missing at least one tooth. She gestures to the chair under the door.*)

What's all this? Expecting an army?

(**PRESENT** *moves the chair away.*)

ELEANOR. I didn't know what to expect.

PRESENT. *(Dances a jig.)* And look what you got. You must have been a really good girl 'dis year.

ELEANOR. I don't celebrate Christmas.

PRESENT. No?

ELEANOR. No.

PRESENT. Chanukah?

(**ELEANOR** *shakes her head "no."*)

PRESENT. Kwanzaa?

(**ELEANOR** *shakes her head "no."*)

Cinco de Mayo?

(**ELEANOR** *gives Present a look.*)

Well, you definitely could stand to celebrate somethin'.

(**PRESENT** *takes out a flask, offers it to* **ELEANOR**. **ELEANOR** *shakes her head "no," appalled.*)

PRESENT. Go on. Go on.

ELEANOR. I don't drink.

PRESENT. You do now.

>(**ELEANOR** *hesitates. She takes the flask. She takes a sip. She seems to like it.*)

PRESENT. Tasty, ain't it?

ELEANOR. What is it?

PRESENT. Me own special blend of goodness. Makes all who drinks of it, charitable and...generous.

>(**PRESENT** *takes a good look at* **ELEANOR**.)

It's gonna take more than a sip for you.

>(**PRESENT** *takes the flask back. She surveys the office.*)

Past been 'ere?

ELEANOR. Yes.

PRESENT. Great. Always screws things up when I arrive first.

>(**ELEANOR** *nods, still very frightened.*)

And the other one. The big guy. He been through?

>(**ELEANOR** *shakes her head.*)

You think I'm bad, wait 'til you lay eyes on 'im. Serious bloke, 'e is. Bloody awful temper. *(She smiles)* A real angel of death.

ELEANOR. Right.

PRESENT. No, 'e is! The *real* angel of death.

>(**ELEANOR** *cowers.* **PRESENT** *crosses to the wall and offers her hand.*)

So. You ready?

ELEANOR. For what?

PRESENT. Take my hand.

>(**ELEANOR** *hesitates.*)

Come on. Come on. I don't bite.

>(**ELEANOR** *takes* **PRESENT**'s *hand.* **PRESENT** *smiles.*)

Much. Brace yourself

>(*A large sucking sound followed by a small pop is heard*

as **PRESENT** *pulls* **ELEANOR** *through the wall. In the darkness, we hear "Oh, Christmas Tree" being sung on the opposite side of the stage.)*

ELEANOR. Who's that singing?

PRESENT. See fer yerself.

*(***PRESENT*** snaps her fingers. Nothing happens.)*

ELEANOR. I can't see anything.

PRESENT. Ah, bloody hell.

*(***PRESENT*** snaps her fingers again. Nothing happens. She snaps again. She jumps around, snapping violently. The lights flicker on.)*

PRESENT. Seems everything's a bit off. Been meaning to get me'self greased…and tightened.

ELEANOR. Is that my nephew? Phillip?

PRESENT. That be the one. And his new bride. Remember her name?

ELEANOR. Carla.

PRESENT. Middle initial?

ELEANOR. A. For Annoying.

PRESENT. She ain't real fond of you neither. And for good reason, I'm told.

ELEANOR. What reason?

PRESENT. Recognize the other two?

ELEANOR. No.

PRESENT. Friends of the lad. Friends.

*(***PRESENT*** smiles.)*

You familiar with 'at term?

*(***ELEANOR*** glares at ***PRESENT*** [she's not so afraid anymore]. ***PRESENT*** blows her nose with her dress.)*

I love this one. A real jerker. Always gets me.

ELEANOR. Why are we…?

(The song ends.)

PRESENT. Shhh. The lad's about to say somethin'.

ELEANOR. Stop calling him that. He's a full-grown...

PRESENT. Hush!

LISA. You miss doing musicals, Phil?

PHIL. Oh, God, no.

LISA. Why? You were good. You should get back into it.

(Phil laughs.)

PHIL. I hated it. Except in high school. With Billyboy here.

BILL. Please. I never had to sing. I was only a walk-on.

LISA. *(Hugging* **BILL***)* You never told me you were an actor.

BILL. Well, I wasn't a pro. Like this guy.

PHIL. Stop.

CARLA. The only reason Phil did musicals to begin with is because his Aunt shipped him off to summer camp. So she wouldn't have to deal with him.

*(**PRESENT** looks at **ELEANOR**, appalled.)*

PRESENT. Oh, my.

*(**PRESENT** gives **ELEANOR** a dirty look.)*

ELEANOR. It was a very expensive camp.

PHIL. If she hadn't, I never would have discovered London and we never would have met.

CARLA. No, no. She gets no credit for that. If it was up to her, we...

PHIL. Come on. She likes you.

*(**CARLA** laughs. **PRESENT** laughs as well.)*

LISA. What's so funny?

CARLA. At our wedding she had her car service idle in front of the church so she could drop off the gift and go.

BILL. She's loaded, right?

LISA. What did she give you?

CARLA. Salad bowls.

LISA. Crystal?

CARLA. Plastic. You know that plastic wood with the criss-crosses? From like 1975?

ELEANOR. They were very retro.

BILL. Oh, my.

LISA. She's that bad?

CARLA/PRESENT. Worse.

PHIL. She has a few good traits.

CARLA/LISA. Name one./Do tell.

PHIL. She's…she has…she's…very

(Laughter.)

CARLA. Controlling?

PRESENT. *(Shouting to the couples.)* That's right!

LISA. Passive aggressive?

PRESENT. You tell 'em!

ELEANOR. Stop it.

BILL. Well, maybe if she's so rich, she'll get you something nice for Christmas.

CARLA. Please. The only thing Phil ever asked her to give him was his mother's engagement ring. For me.

LISA. Did she?

CARLA. Are you kidding? Scrooge probably hocked it.

PHIL. Let's stop this. How 'bout we toast her?

(Lifts his glass.)

To Aunt Eleanor.

*(**LISA** and **BILL** raise their glasses as well. **CARLA** doesn't move. **ELEANOR** tries to lift **CARLA**'s arm.)*

CARLA. I'm sorry, honey.

PHIL. It's Christmas.

CARLA. I don't care. If your grandmother hadn't lived as long as she had, you would have ended up in an orphanage.

LISA/PRESENT. My god, really?/'Dat right?

*(**CARLA** pokes **PHIL**. Present pokes **ELEANOR**.)*

CARLA/PRESENT. Tell them./Tell me.

*(**PHIL** nods ["It's true."].)*

CARLA. I would do anything for you, Honey.

    (**CARLA** *kisses* **PHIL.**)

Except toast that woman.

PHIL. I guess I feel bad for her.

BILL. Why?

PHIL. Well, I invited her for drinks tonight. And dinner tomorrow.

LISA. Is she coming?

    (**CARLA** *wildly shakes her head "no."*)

Too bad. I would have loved to have met this creature.

ELEANOR. Creature?

LISA. Sounds like a fantastic case study.

CARLA. Oh, I would pay to see her cowering on your couch.

LISA. I could psychoanalyze her and then you could prosecute her for all her evil deeds.

BILL. Why isn't she coming?

PHIL. She's working.

BILL. On Christmas?

PHIL. She has no one in her life, except the poor lady who works for her.

CARLA. Who we also invited.

LISA. Did she accept?

CARLA. No. She's going through a really difficult time?

PHIL. Her son is very ill.

BILL. Is she married?

PHIL. Divorced.

CARLA. And with what Scrooge pays her, it's amazing what she's been able to do.

LISA. How 'bout we toast *her*?

    (**CARLA** *raises her glass.*)

CARLA. Now Bobbie I'll toast to.

    (**PHIL** *raises his glass.*)

PHIL. And Timmy. To Bobbie and Timmy.

(**BILL** *and* **LISA** *raise their glasses.* **PRESENT** *pulls the flask out of her Christmas garb and hands it to* **ELEANOR**. *The two couples clink glasses.* **ELEANOR** *shoots back a drink [a healthy swig].*)

CARLA. Who's ready for plum pudding?

LISA. I'll have a slice of pecan pie

BILL. What about my red velvet cupcakes?

(*The look at him blankly and start out.*)

PRESENT. (*Yanking the flask away from* **ELEANOR**.) She who hogs the feast for herself chokes on it.

ELEANOR. Excuse me?

PRESENT. Annoyin', isn't it?

(**PRESENT** *snaps her finger. The lights rise on* **BOBBIE** *in front of a Christmas tree. A glass of milk and a plate of cookies is next to her on the floor.* **PRESENT** *walks up to* **BOBBIE**. **BOBBIE** *doesn't see her.* **PRESENT** *roughly strokes* **BOBBIE**'s *head.*)

She's a real class act, 'dis one…Like me.

TIMMY. (*From offstage*) Mom?

(**BOBBIE** *quickly puts the gift behind the tree to hide it.* **TIMMY** *lumbers in. He is in pajamas. He wears glasses.*)

BOBBIE. What are you doing up?

TIMMY. I can't sleep.

BOBBIE. You excited?

TIMMY. My tummy hurts.

BOBBIE. Well, you didn't have much for dinner. You need to eat with the medicine, honey. To help digest it.

TIMMY. You told me I could take new medicine. That wouldn't make me feel sick.

BOBBIE. I just have to wait until the vouchers go through. It won't be much longer. I promise.

TIMMY. Can I have one of those cookies?

BOBBIE. Wouldn't you rather finish your hamburger?

(**TIMMY** *shakes his head "no."*)

Green beans?

(**TIMMY** *shakes his head "no."*)

Okay.

(**BOBBIE** *hands* **TIMMY** *a cookie from the plate.*)

Only because it's Christmas. And you've been such a good boy this year.

TIMMY. You can have the other one if you want. There really isn't a Santa Claus.

BOBBIE. What? Who told you that?

TIMMY. Peter Brandon.

BOBBIE. Well, Peter Brandon doesn't know what he's talking about.

TIMMY. So, there is a Santa?

BOBBIE. Of course.

TIMMY. Prove it…*(A beat.)* Just kidding.

(**BOBBIE** *tickles* **TIMMY**.)

BOBBIE. Better?

(**TIMMY** *smiles, nods.*)

You want some milk?

TIMMY. No. Better leave it for Santa. Just in case.

BOBBIE. Good idea.

TIMMY. I've really been good, Mom?

BOBBIE. Are you kidding? You've been great.

PRESENT. A prince.

BOBBIE. You're the bravest boy I've ever known. You know that?

TIMMY. Ever?

(**BOBBIE** *nods "yes."*)

Ever and ever?

(**BOBBIE** *laughs and nods.*)

So brave that you'll let me play soccer again?

BOBBIE. Well, when you're feeling better, and the doctor says it's okay to play, then…

(**TIMMY** *looks down.*)

ELEANOR. Why won't she let the kid play soccer? What kind of doctor…?

PRESENT. Why don't you put a stocking in it? If you shut your piehole and opened your ears just once, you might learn a thing or two.

TIMMY. Mom? The kids at school…they…

BOBBIE. What?

TIMMY. Do I have to keep going to school, Mom?

BOBBIE. Timmy, what's going on?

TIMMY. Mom…my tick-tock…can they fix it?

(**BOBBIE** *hugs* **TIMMY**.)

ELEANOR. Can they?

PRESENT. I reckon it's possible. If she can find another job in time.

ELEANOR. Another job?

PRESENT. With a boss that ain't so cheap. Otherwise, there ain't much hope, I'm afraid. Poor lad's saddled with a bit of a time bomb.

BOBBIE. Now off to bed. Santa won't come if he knows you're awake.

(**TIMMY** *rises excitedly.*)

TIMMY. I bet since I've been so good, Santa's gonna bring me a new Wii. With like a million games to play on it.

BOBBIE. Honey, Santa…he might…he might wait until next year to give you something like that…

TIMMY. But all the other kids have one and…

BOBBIE. Come here.

(**BOBBIE** *takes him in her arms and hugs him hard.*)

I love you so much.

ELEANOR. What's a "Wii"?

PRESENT. Some sort of massive board game, I reckon.

(PRESENT *glares at* ELEANOR.)

A giant contraption that Bo'bie clearly can't afford.

TIMMY. Mom?

BOBBIE. Yeah?

TIMMY. I can't breathe.

(BOBBIE *smiles and releases* TIMMY.)

BOBBIE. How's your tum?

TIMMY. *(Smiles.)* Better.

BOBBIE. Sweet dreams.

(TIMMY *starts out. He stops and turns back to* BOBBIE.)

TIMMY. Will you sing me a Christmas carol? To help me sleep?

BOBBIE. I can't…I can't sing. Timmy.

TIMMY. Yes, you can. I love it when you sing.

(TIMMY *pulls on Bobbie's arm.*)

Come on. Come on!

BOBBIE. Timmy!… To bed. Now.

(TIMMY *exits.*))

PRESENT. Lovely lad. Would have made quite the gentleman.

ELEANOR. Would have? You mean…?

PRESENT. What do you care?

ELEANOR. Are you implying that I…?

PRESENT. Why *sure*…with the little runt out of the way, Bobbie won't have anything to go home to. You can work her twenty-four-seven, Mistress Scrooge!

ELEANOR. No, I wouldn't ever wish that on…

(ELEANOR*'s office phone rings, causing* ELEANOR *to jump.*)

ELEANOR. Who is that?...Who's calling me?!

(**ELEANOR** *cowers.*)

It's the third spirit, isn't it? The Big One.

PRESENT. Not likely. He wouldn't call. Doesn't say much.

ELEANOR. Then?

(*The lights bump up on* **JOHN**, *standing in the area where* **PHIL, CARLA, LISA,** *and* **BILL** *were standing. The phone continues to ring.*)

JOHN. Answer the phone, Scrooge. I know you're there. Answer the phone!

ELEANOR. (*Quietly.*) Should I answer it?

(**JOHN** *begins pacing.*)

PRESENT. Your call.

(**PRESENT** *smiles.*)

JOHN. You can't ignore me, Scrooge. I'm not going to give up.

(*He screams into the phone.*)

You hear me?! SCROOOOOGE!

(**JOHN** *flips his cell phone shut. The phone stops ringing.*)

PRESENT. That bloke your lover?

ELEANOR. No!

PRESENT. He seems a bit off. What'd you do to 'im, anyway?

(**JOHN** *dials another number.*)

ELEANOR. Nothing. It was business. Strictly business.

JOHN. Hi...It's John Misslehouse. Yes, Merry Christmas. She's fine. He's fine. Look, I'm sorry...Is Brian in? Actually, it is...It's Eleanor Scrooge. She's launched a takeover. I'm sorry to have to call on Christmas Eve with this. I still can't wrap my mind around it. My family...they...It is so...

(**JOHN** *bends over. He staggers. He collapses. A beat.*

JOHN *lies motionless.* ELEANOR *and* PRESENT *look at each other. They look back at* JOHN.)

ELEANOR. What did you do?

PRESENT. Me?

(ELEANOR *slowly approaches* JOHN. PRESENT *follows her. They stand over* JOHN *for a moment.* PRESENT *picks up* JOHN*'s arm and then lets it fall to the floor.*)

PRESENT. Ah, rotten luck.

ELEANOR. What now?

(PRESENT *shrugs.*)

PRESENT. Why don't you tell him one of your bloody awful sayin's. That should drive the last nail in.

(ELEANOR *looks at* PRESENT, *panicked.*)

ELEANOR. Do something!

PRESENT. Try shaking him. See if he moves.

(ELEANOR *kneels down by* JOHN. *She nudges him.* PRESENT *takes out her flask.*)

ELEANOR. You know anything about CPR?

PRESENT. Nope. Back in my day, we'd bleed 'em, or gave 'em herbs. Dry root and such. Here…

(PRESENT *hands* ELEANOR *her flask.*)

Get the spirits working for you.

(ELEANOR *takes a swig from the flask.*)

Not you…'em!

(ELEANOR *pours a sip into* JOHN*'s mouth. A slight smile exudes from his mouth.*)

Ah, there's a bit of life in 'em. But not much.

(ELEANOR *starts to awkwardly push on* JOHN*'s chest. No reaction from* JOHN. ELEANOR *then starts pounding on his chest.*)

PRESENT. Are you trying to save him or kill him?

ELEANOR. He needs mouth-to-mouth… help me!

PRESENT. As much as I'd love to, I ain't got no oxygen inside me. Just cold air. Plus, I ain't brushed my teeth in over 200 years.

ELEANOR. I don't think I can.

PRESENT. His life is in your hands, love.

ELEANOR. *(Looking around.)* Help!

PRESENT. Best hurry now.

ELEANOR. And if I don't?

PRESENT. I'm thinking I'll turn you into a stink bug. Or the head of a skunk on the arse of a pig. Maybe a rat… cat. Or a slug…with paws…and wings! No…stink bug suits you.

*(**ELEANOR** puts her mouth on **JOHN**'s. She blows. Nothing. She repeats the process. **JOHN** does not stir.)*

ELEANOR. Help me.

*(**PRESENT** shrugs.)*

Please.

*(**PRESENT** begins snapping wildly. Nothing happens. She licks her finger and concentrates. She snaps again. The lights go out.)*

Help me!

*(The lights flicker back in **ELEANOR**'s office. There is a soft glow that rises on **ELEANOR**, still kneeling on the floor. John is no longer underneath her. **PRESENT** has disappeared. **ELEANOR** sits up quickly, looking for **JOHN**'s body. **ELEANOR** quickly rises. She jerks her head.)*

Oww.

*(**ELEANOR** jerks the other side of her head.)*

Oww. What the…?

(She realizes. She slowly reaches up to her head, feeling the tiny horns starting to break through.)

No!

(She rushes into the office. She closes the door, revealing **FUTURE**, *who was standing behind it. He is a tall and imposing figure.* **ELEANOR** *sits in her chair and grabs the phone receiver.)*

Security?

(The phone is dead. **ELEANOR** *hits numerous buttons, trying to get a dial tone. She moves the receiver back to her face.)*

Security?!

(The phone remains dead. **ELEANOR** *hangs up the phone and grabs her purse off the floor. She fumbles through it.)*

Where is my cell phone?

*(**ELEANOR** rises and heads toward the coat rack, running into Future.* **ELEANOR** *starts searching through* **FUTURE**'s *overcoat, thinking it is her coat. She can't find the pockets. She looks around and then slowly moves her head up and sees the face of* **FUTURE** *(in a black overcoat, biker boots, and sunglasses).* **ELEANOR** *screams and backs up, falling over her desk.* **ELEANOR** *peers up from behind her desk.)*

ELEANOR. Are you...the third advisor?

*(**FUTURE** slowly nods "yes.")*

Are you here to show me something?

*(**FUTURE** slowly nods "yes.")*

Can't you just tell me? I'll listen. I swear.

*(**FUTURE** slowly points into the dark reception area.* **ELEANOR** *feels her head.)*

What can I do to make these go away?

(Annoyed, **FUTURE** *aggressively jabs his extended finger toward the reception area.* **ELEANOR** *slowly rises. She moves toward the reception area. As* **ELEANOR** *approaches the reception area, the lights slowly rise to reveal* **NELLIE** *at* **BOBBIE**'s *desk.* **NELLIE** *is filing her*

nails. She wears a multi-colored Santa hat. **ELEANOR** *enters the reception area.* **FUTURE** *follows her in.)*

ELEANOR. Cratchit?

*(***ELEANOR*** moves to ***NELLIE.****)*

Thank God, I've had the worst nightmare…

*(***ELEANOR*** sees that it is ***NELLIE.****)*

Who are you? What are you doing sitting at…

(The phone rings. **NELLIE** *snatches it up.)*

NELLIE. Scrooge and Kunkle.

ELEANOR. *(To* **FUTURE.***)* Scrooge and who?

*(***FUTURE*** brings his finger to his face, indicating for ***ELEANOR*** to be quiet.)*

NELLIE. Yes…No, Roberta doesn't work here anymore. I mean, she does, but she's been out for about six months. Bereavement leave.

ELEANOR. Bereavement?

NELLIE. I'm the temp. We'll not so temp anymore. Uh-huh, well Eleanor seems to be very popular…you're not the first collection company that's called…I wish I could help you but…

*(***JUAN*** enters with a four pack box of wine. He is dressed in a brightly colored suit and disco boots.* **NELLIE** *smiles and waves at him.)*

Can you hold on a second? Thanks.

*(***NELLIE*** rises.)*

Hola, Baby.

*(***JUAN*** pretends he is a bull fighter, waving his cape for ***NELLIE*** to charge.* **NELLIE** *pretends she is a bull and then rushes toward* **JUAN.** *Eleanor gets stuck in between* **JUAN** *and* **NELLIE** *as they embrace.* **JUAN** *kisses* **NEL-LIE**'s neck. Eleanor squirms out from between them, disgusted.)*

Stop…Stop! I'm working.

JUAN. Is…La Loca in?

    *(**ELEANOR** gasps.)*

ELEANOR. Did that creature just call me…

NELLIE. No, she's out.

    (Laughs.)

    As per usual.

ELEANOR. Out?? I'm never out.

JUAN. Mind if I…how do you say…surf de turf?

    *(**NELLIE** smiles, waves him toward **ELEANOR**'s office.*
    ***JUAN** heads for **ELEANOR**'s office with a box of wine.)*

    What's her…how do you say…password?

NELLIE. Search and Destroy. All one word.

JUAN. Excellente.

ELEANOR. How did she get my…?

NELLIE. You still there?…Hello?

    *(**NELLIE** hangs up the phone. The phone rings again.*
    ***JUAN** turns on the computer.)*

    Hey, Sven. What's up, lover?…Really?

    *(**JUAN** opens the box of wine and smells the bouquet.)*

NELLIE. How long ago?…Why didn't you stop him?

ELEANOR. What site is that? Are those people…?

    *(**JUAN** puts his feet up on the desk.)*

    Oh, gross.

    *(To **FUTURE**.)*

    Are you just going to let him do that?

NELLIE. Okay… You're the best… See you tonight… And
    Sven?… don't forget your Gladiator outfit.

    *(**NELLIE** barks and hangs up the phone. She speaks into*
    the intercom.)

    Juan?… Juan!

JUAN. Speak to me.

NELLIE. We have a visitor.

JUAN. A visitor? We never get…how do you say…visitors.

NELLIE. You better hide.

JUAN. Bueno.

(*JUAN hides under the desk.* **NELLIE** *quickly clears off her desk. She takes her Christmas hat off and stuffs it in a drawer. She sits straight up and pretends like she is typing on the computer.* **MR**. **BENSON**, *dressed in an overcoat and suit, enters the office.*)

NELLIE. Good morning.

BENSON. Is this Scrooge and Marley?

NELLIE. Scrooge and…Kunkle.

BENSON. Are you Ms. Scrooge?

(**NELLIE** *laughs.*)

NELLIE. No, sir. I'm Nellie Kunkle. Pleased to meet…

BENSON. Is Ms. Scrooge in?

NELLIE. Not presently, no.

BENSON. Do you expect her in soon?

NELLIE. No, I don't. She's been out sick for awhile now.

ELEANOR. Not true. I never get ill.

BENSON. Can you sign on her behalf?

NELLIE. Sure.

(**BENSON** *holds out a document.*)

ELEANOR. Don't!

BENSON. Here.

(**NELLIE** *signs.*)

And here…And here.

(**NELLIE** *signs.* **BENSON** *hands her an official document.*)

Good day.

(**BENSON** *starts out.*)

NELLIE. Wait. What is this?

BENSON. It's an eviction notice.

NELLIE/ELEANOR. Eviction?

BENSON. You have 24 hours to vacate the premises.

NELLIE. Vacate. Why?

BENSON. The company was bought out. Scrooge and Marley...

NELLIE. Kunkle.

BENSON. ...no longer exists.

NELLIE. But how can that be? Ms. Scrooge is worth millions.

BENSON. Millions? The stock has dropped 95% since Thanksgiving. This was a mercy takeover. Necessity is the mother of invention.

(**ELEANOR** *and* **NELLIE** *gasp together.*)

NELLIE. What am I supposed to do?

BENSON. Not my problem.

NELLIE. *(She saddles up to him.)* Can I help you with something?

BENSON. Huh?

NELLIE. You need a temp?

BENSON. No.

NELLIE. But...

BENSON. Happy holidays.

(*Benson exits.* **NELLIE** *is shocked. She pushes the intercom.*)

Juan?

(**JUAN** *leaps up.*)

JUAN. Is the Coast...how do you say...clear?

NELLIE. You better come out here.

(**JUAN** *comes out to the reception area.* **NELLIE** *gathers her things off the desk and holds them in her arms.*)

ELEANOR. How can this be? I made Scrooge, Inc. takeover-proof.

(**FUTURE** *points to* **NELLIE** *and* **JUAN**.)

This was my life. My legacy.

JUAN. Did the...how do you say...visitor come?

(**JUAN** *takes* **NELLIE** *in his arms and kisses her neck.*)

NELLIE. Yes…We just got evicted…We have to leave.

(**JUAN** *abruptly stops kissing* **NELLIE**. *He grabs his boxes of wine and exits.*)

JUAN. Adios.

NELLIE. Juan?…Juanito!

(**NELLIE** *rushes out, after him.*)

ELEANOR. I don't understand. I never would have left those deviants alone in my office.

(**FUTURE** *points in the opposite direction. A light comes up on* **BOBBIE**.*)

ELEANOR. Roberta? What is she doing on the ground?

BOBBIE. Good morning, Timmy. I have something for you.

(**BOBBIE** *takes out a Christmas card.*)

It's a Christmas card. Your teacher sent it. Your class made it at school.

(*She reads.*)

It says…Dear Ms. Cratchit, We wanted to tell you that we miss Timmy very much. We think of him a lot, especially when we play after school. We won the county final this year and we dedicated the game to Timmy. He was very nice and the coolest boy in class. We want you to know that we will never forget him. He will always be our…friend. We hope we can play with Timmy again someday…in heaven.

(*A beat.* **BOBBIE** *looks up*)

The sky is cloudy, Tim…but it's still a beautiful day… And quiet.

(*A beat. She closes her eyes.*)

So quiet.

(**BOBBIE** *looks around. She reaches down and touches the earth above* **TIMMY**'s *grave. She sings the first few verses of "All Through the Night," very softly at first and* *then stronger as she gains confidence.)*

Merry Christmas, Sweetheart.

(A loud clap of thunder. **BOBBIE** *looks up, puts the card in the bag and exits. Lights fade on* **BOBBIE**. **PHIL** *enters with the* **GRAVEDIGGER**. **PHIL** *is holding flowers.)*

ELEANOR. Phillip? Did Phillip know Timmy?

GRAVEDIGGER. This be the stop. Once the mourners arrive, I'll bring the body out.

PHIL. No need to wait.

GRAVEDIGGER. Huh?

PHIL. You can…commence.

GRAVEDIGGER. It's no problem. I got her on ice.

PHIL. It's just me.

GRAVEDIGGER. Huh?

PHIL. There are no other mourners.

GRAVEDIGGER. Really? I thought she was some high-powered broad.

ELEANOR. She?

PHIL. She was. But not actually…admired.

ELEANOR. Who are they talking about? Say something!

GRAVEDIGGER. Rich?

PHIL. She was.

GRAVEDIGGER. Huh?

PHIL. SHE WAS RICH!

GRAVEDIGGER. Wow. That's rough. Doesn't matter now, huh? Can't take it with you.

(A loud clap of thunder is heard.)

GRAVEDIGGER. Storm's coming.

PHIL. Yeah.

GRAVEDIGGER. *(Looking up.)* Better go inside 'til it passes.

PHIL. Can't we just get this over with?

GRAVEDIGGER. No can do. I've already been struck once out here. Not taking another chance. She ain't going anywhere.

*(Another clap of thunder. **GRAVEDIGGER** takes the flowers from **PHIL** and throws them in the grave. He runs off, pulling **PHIL** with him. **ELEANOR** slowly moves closer to the stone. She gasps. She turns to **FUTURE**.)*

ELEANOR. No. This can't be. I'm not ready. I have too much left to do.

*(**FUTURE** moves toward **ELEANOR**.)*

Please. I'll make amends. I'll be better. Much better.

*(**FUTURE** points into the grave.)*

Give me another chance. I'm begging you.

*(**FUTURE** reaches his hand up to **ELEANOR**.)*

I'm not ready.

*(**FUTURE** pushes **ELEANOR** into the grave.)*

I'm not ready!

*(Blackout. We hear several claps of thunder and see lighting flash across the stage as **FUTURE** stands in front of **ELEANOR**'s grave. Lights up on **PAST** on the opposite side of the stage. He laughs hysterically and then stops. He snaps his finger. Lights out on **PAST** and up on **PRESENT**. She laughs hysterically. She stops. She snaps her finger. The Lights out on **PRESENT** and up on **FUTURE**. He stands stone faced for a long moment facing us. Finally a small single "ha" escapes him. Lights out on **FUTURE** and slowly up on **ELEANOR**, head hunched over on her desk.)*

ELEANOR. No… No… NO!!!

*(**ELEANOR** wakes with a start and leaps back in her chair, causing it to roll against the wall. She slowly gets out of the chair and looks around. She calls in a whisper)*

ELEANOR. Jacob?

(She slowly opens the curtains. It is a clear and beautiful Christmas morning (snowing if technically possible). She

crosses to her door and calls out.)

Past?

(She crosses to the swivel chair and swings it around.)

Present?

(She crosses to the coat rack.)

Mr. Angel of Death?

(A beat as she looks out.)

I'm alive. I'm still here!

(She looks up. She smiles.)

Thank you.

(She looks out the window. She considers. She puts on her coat. She takes the bin of cookies out of the trash can and puts them on her desk. She picks up the receiver to her phone.)

ELEANOR. *(While eating a cookie)* Good morning!..Is this Sven? It's Eleanor. Eleanor Scrooge. From the 16th floor. No, nothing's wrong. What day is it?…I was hoping you'd say that…Can you order some things for me?…No, Not coffee…Cider and cookies, enough for a group…Charge them to my account…Great! I'll bring down a list…Oh, and I'll need you to place a few calls for me. To a few friends…I'll make it worth your while, I promise you…Yes, Eleanor Scrooge…No, I feel fine. I feel quite wonderful, actually…I'll be right down. I'm going shopping!

(She starts to put down the phone but stops. She quickly brings the receiver back to her ear)

Oh, and Sven?…Merry Christmas!

*(Blackout. We hear church chimes. When the lights rise, the **CAROLERS** are back in front of Bobbie's empty desk. The stage is brightly lit. The **CAROLERS** half-heartedly sing "Deck the Halls" They read the paper, swivel in **BOBBIE**'s chair, text message, etc. The carol ends.)*

CAROLER 1. We should have asked her to pay us in advance.

She's off her rocker.

CAROLER 2. I don't think it's her. Must be a twin sister.

CAROLER 3. No, it's her.

CAROLER 4. Is she really going to pay us each a thousand dollars? Just to sing Christmas carols?

CAROLER 2. That's what she said.

CAROLER 1. Well? Should we keep singing?

CAROLER 2. I guess.

CAROLER 4. But there's no one here.

CAROLER 3. Who cares. I need the money.

(The **CAROLERS** *sing "I Saw Three Ships Come Sailing In." For the last verse,* **ELEANOR** *enters the office and sings with the group (who are frightened to say the least). She carries a garment bag. Two* **TECHNICIANS***, dressed in black Santa hats, then enter with a platter of Christmas cookies and a large punch bowl of cider.)*

ELEANOR. Brilliant! What a perfect song for Christmas!

(To technicians.)

Here. The desk is fine.

(The **TECHNICIANS** *put the cider and cookies on* **BOBBIE***'s desk.* **ELEANOR** *gives them both a large handful of cash bills.)*

Here you are.

TECHNICIANS. Thank you!

ELEANOR. You're welcome. Merry Christmas!

TECHNICIANS. Merry Christmas!

(The **TECHNICIANS** *rush out, overjoyed.)*

Hot cider and treats for all!

*(***ELEANOR** *checks the thermostat.)*

ELEANOR. Is it getting warmer in here?

CAROLER 2. *(Taking off his cap.)* Oh, yes, Ma'am. Thank you.

*(***ELEANOR** *starts off toward her office.)*

ELEANOR. Oh, shoot.

(She crosses to the door.)

I meant to order a case of champagne.

CAROLER 4. I'll go.

ELEANOR. You sure?

CAROLER 4. If you know of some place open.

CAROLER 1. My cousin owns a store. Don't know if he'd open up though.

ELEANOR. *(ELEANOR hands her a few large bills)* Would this convince him?

CAROLER 1. Yep.

(CAROLER 1 snatches the money.)

ELEANOR. The finest you can buy.

CAROLER 1/CAROLER 4. Yes, Ma'am!

(CAROLER 1 and CAROLER 4 rush out. ELEANOR heads toward her office.)

ELEANOR. I'll be right back. Keep singing!

(ELEANOR rushes off into the office with her garment bag into her private bathroom. The remaining two CAROLERS look at each other in shock. They sing "Hark the Herald Angels Sing." PHIL and CARLA enter. They see the CAROLERS. PHIL looks at the glass door to make sure he walked into the right suite.)

PHIL. Excuse me. Is this the 16th Floor?

CAROLER 2. Yes, sir.

CARLA. The office of Eleanor Scrooge?

CAROLER 3. That's right. Cider?

CARLA. What's going on, Phil?

PHIL. I have no idea.

(To CAROLERS.)

Is Bobbie here?

CAROLER 2. Who?

(BOBBIE and TIMMY enter.)

BOBBIE. Phil?

PHIL. Hi, Bobbie.

BOBBIE. *(Shocked.)* What in the world? How did they get in?

PHIL. I was hoping you'd tell me.

BOBBIE. I got a call this morning. From security. They said it was an emergency.

PHIL. Us, too.

TIMMY. Look, Mom. Christmas cookies!

BOBBIE. Hold on, Timmy… Where is Ms. Scrooge?

PHIL. I have no idea. We just got here.

(**TIMMY** *rushes to the cookies.*)

BOBBIE. Timmy!

TIMMY. Mom, can I have a cookie?

(**SARAH** *and* **BEN** *enter.*)

SARAH/BEN. Good morning!

BOBBIE. Hello…What are you…?

SARAH. Ms. Scrooge invited us.

BOBBIE. Invited you?

BEN. Said our services were needed immediately.

CARLA. Services?

(**SARAH** *and* **BEN** *turn and look at* **CARLA** *and* **PHIL.**)

SARAH/BEN. Happy Holidays!

SARAH. My name is Sarah. And this is Ben.

(**BEN** *nods, smiles.*)

BEN. We're volunteers for the Manhattan Coalition for Humanity.

SARAH/BEN. Homeless helpers!

CAROLER 3. Should we keep singing?

CAROLER 2. I guess.

(*The* **CAROLERS** *begin to sing "Joy to the World" as* **SARAH** *and* **BEN** *continue*)

BEN. At this time of year…

SARAH. With temperatures hovering around the freezing point…

BEN. The homeless population is facing a daily struggle for survival.

SARAH. It is up to our citizens…

BOBBIE. Excuse me…

(The **CAROLERS** *continue to sing.)*

BEN. The leaders of our fair city…

SARAH. To ensure that these unfortunate souls have the support they need to…

BOBBIE. Excuse me!

(The carolers and **SARAH** *and* **BEN** *stop abruptly and look at* **BOBBIE.***)*

I'm sorry. Very sorry, but…you all have to go.

*(***ELEANOR** *appears in a full Santa Claus outfit, complete with the beard and wig, hat and gloves.)*

ELEANOR. Ho Ho Ho, Merry Christmas!!

*(***BOBBIE** *gasps.* **TIMMY** *smiles.)*

TIMMY. Look, Mom, it's Santa Claus!

*(***BOBBIE** *crosses to her phone and picks it up.)*

PHIL. What are you doing?

BOBBIE. Calling security.

PHIL. Right. Good idea.

TIMMY. Thank you, Santa.

*(***ELEANOR** *crosses to* **TIMMY.** *She has a big red bag with her.)*

ELEANOR. For what, Timmy?

TIMMY. For my new Christmas sweater.

CARLA. Wait.

*(***BOBBIE** *stops dialing.)*

He called him Timmy. He knows his name.

(BOBBIE hangs up the phone.)

TIMMY. Mom said Ms. Claus knitted it special. 'Cause I was good this year.

ELEANOR. That's true. And because you were *so* good, you get another present. Something extra special.

BOBBIE. Excuse me. Could I speak with you a moment, please?

ELEANOR. Patience, lass. I have something for you, too, don't fret.

BOBBIE. Me?

(ELEANOR hands TIMMY a present.)

ELEANOR. Here you go, Timmy.

(TIMMY grabs the gift and opens it with a flourish. It is a Wii game system.)

TIMMY. *(Turns and holds it up for BOBBIE to see.)* Look, Mom, a Wii!

(BOBBIE crosses to TIMMY.)

BOBBIE. *(To TIMMY.)* Yes.

(TIMMY hugs BOBBIE. BOBBIE holds him tight. ELEANOR crosses to SARAH and BEN.)

ELEANOR. Ho Ho Ho! If it isn't the Happy Homewreckers.

SARAH/BEN. Homeless Helpers!

ELEANOR. Whatever. Here.

(ELEANOR hands SARAH an envelope. SARAH and BEN open it together. They hold up the check.)

SARAH/BEN. Oh my god!

ELEANOR. That should cover a few bricks for your new shelter.

SARAH. This should cover all the bricks.

BEN. And then some.

SARAH/BEN. Thanks… Santa.

(JOHN enters.)

JOHN. *(To* PHIL.*)* Excuse me. I'm looking for Ms. Scrooge.
It's urgent.

PHIL. So am I.

ELEANOR. *(Looking up.)* John?

JOHN. Is that Santa Claus?

BOBBIE. *(Sincerely.)* I think it very well might be.

ELEANOR. John!

> (ELEANOR *rushes to* JOHN.)

You're okay!

> (ELEANOR *hugs* JOHN. JOHN *is totally confused and*
> *does not hug* ELEANOR *[Santa] back.)*

When you collapsed last night. I thought you were
dead.

JOHN. Yes, well…

> *(Looks around sheepishly.)*

I have panic attacks…They…I faint sometimes. How
did you know that I…

ELEANOR. *(She hands him a card.)* Here. Open it…Go on.

> (JOHN *opens the card.)*

It's twenty thousand shares of Misslehouse stock. It
makes you a majority owner. No one can ever take the
company from you now.

JOHN. But…Scrooge. She…

ELEANOR. That old humbug? We had a long talk.

> (ELEANOR *takes out a letter rolled up and tied with a*
> *red ribbon.)*

Here. Read this. It says she relinquishes all control of
Misslehouse holdings to you.

JOHN. *(Reading.)* How in the world did you…You are Santa
Claus, aren't you?

ELEANOR. Have some cider, my good man.

> (ELEANOR *crosses to* PHIL *and* CARLA.*)*

Hello, Carla.

CARLA. *(A bit frightened.)* Hello.

ELEANOR. You been a good girl?

CARLA. I think so.

ELEANOR. I think so, too. And you were right.

CARLA. About what?

ELEANOR. Scrooge. I wouldn't have toasted her, either.

PHIL. Oh, my god.

ELEANOR. *(Hands* **CARLA** *a small unwrapped box.)* Here.

> *(***CARLA** *slowly opens the box. It is* **TESS***'s engagement ring.* **CARLA** *is obviously moved.)*

PHIL. Mother's ring. You are Santa!

CARLA. This isn't Santa.

ALL. IT'S NOT?!

CARLA. No. This is an angel. A Christmas angel.

> *(***ELEANOR** *smiles at* **CARLA***. She starts toward her office.)*

ELEANOR. Cratchit?

BOBBIE. Yes…Santa?

ELEANOR. Follow me. Old Scrooge wants a word with you.

PHIL. She's here?

JOHN. Can I talk to her, too? I'd like to thank her.

ELEANOR. Sorry, gentlemen. Scrooge has some very important business. It needs immediate attention. Official business.

PHIL. But it's Christmas.

BOBBIE. *(To* **PHIL***.)* It's alright. I'll be right back, Timmy.

TIMMY. Okay. Can I have some cider?

> *(***BOBBIE** *smiles and nods.* **TIMMY** *rushes to the cider.* **ELEANOR** *opens the door to the office and lets* **BOBBIE** *in.)*

ELEANOR. Have a seat.

BOBBIE. Where's Ms. Scrooge?

ELEANOR. Patience. Sit.

BOBBIE. She would never let me sit in her…

ELEANOR. Not to worry. Sit.

(**BOBBIE** *sits.*)

Before she comes in, I have something for you, too.

BOBBIE. For me? You don't have to…

(**ELEANOR** *digs through the bag but can't find it.*)

ELEANOR. Now where did I put it.

BOBBIE. That's okay. I don't need anything.

ELEANOR. No. No. I know it's here somewhere.

(**ELEANOR** *remembers. She grabs a card from her suit.*)

Here it is.

(**ELEANOR** *hands* **BOBBIE** *a card.* **BOBBIE** *opens the card and reads it out loud.*)

BOBBIE. An old fool can only make amends with the forgiveness of friends.

(**BOBBIE** *looks at* **ELEANOR** *confused. She looks at the card again and continues to read.*)

P. S. This is the last saying you will ever be subjected to.

(**BOBBIE** *looks at* **ELEANOR** *again.*)

I don't understand.

(**ELEANOR** *nods to the card.* **BOBBIE** *takes a check out from the card.*)

BOBBIE. A blank check? From Ms. Scrooge's personal account…There must be some mistake.

(**BOBBIE** *tries to hand it back.*)

ELEANOR. No mistake.

BOBBIE. It has to be. Ms. Scrooge would never…

ELEANOR. *(In her own voice.)* It's for Timmy.

BOBBIE. Timmy?

(**ELEANOR** *pulls the beard down from her face.*)

Ms. Scrooge?

(ELEANOR smiles at BOBBIE.)

ELEANOR. Take it.

BOBBIE. I don't understand.

ELEANOR. I want you to find out from the doctor how quickly he can schedule the procedure Timmy needs. Tell him cost is no object.

BOBBIE. Ma'am?

(ELEANOR takes the check and folds BOBBIE's hand over it.)

ELEANOR. Merry Christmas, Bobbie.

(BOBBIE begins to cry.)

BOBBIE. Oh, Ma'am. I'm sorry. I…

ELEANOR. Call me Eleanor. Ellie.

(ELEANOR smiles. BOBBIE hugs her. The rest of the cast begins to sing "We Wish You a Merry Christmas." The two pull out of the embrace.)

Why don't you join them? You have a beautiful voice… I'll be right out. Go on.

(BOBBIE crosses to the door.)

BOBBIE. Thank you…Ellie.

(BOBBIE joins the group and starts singing. ELEANOR takes a card out of her desk. It is the card PHIL made ELLIE when he was a little boy. ELEANOR opens it up and stands it on her desk. She smiles. TIMMY crosses to BOBBIE.)

TIMMY. Mom, where's Santa?

(BOBBIE smiles. BOBBIE kneels down to TIMMY and points to the office. She gently pushes TIMMY toward the office. TIMMY runs to the office.)

Santa! Santa!

(ELEANOR hears TIMMY coming and pulls the beard back up. She rises. TIMMY rushes in and takes ELEANOR by the hand. He leads her out, continuing to hold

her hand. **ELEANOR** *and* **TIMMY** *join the group. For the final verse, the* **THREE GHOSTS** *and* **MARLEY** *enter unseen and gather in* **ELEANOR**'s *office. They sing [spiritedly]. They snap their fingers together at the end of the song, sending the stage into blackness. Curtain.)*

End of Play

COSTUMES

ELEANOR #1
Blue Suit
Cream blouse
Blue trouser socks
Black coat
Purse/bag
Black shoes
Blue socks
Glasses on a chain

ELEANOR #2
Santa Jacket
Santa Pants
Santa Hat
Black Boots
Black Belt
White Wig
White Beard on elastic
Body padding
White gloves

BOBBY #1
Glasses
Red/pink scarf
Grey tweed coat
Grey suit jacket
Tan turtleneck sweater
Leg warmers
Grey tights
Sneakers
Black fingerless gloves
Pencils for hair

BOBBY #2
Blue sweater
Grey sweatpants
Socks
Slippers

BOBBY #3
Same as Bobby #1
Black coat
Dark grey scarf

BOBBY #4
Same as Bobby #1

CAROLER #1
Red plaid hat
Green gloves
Red plaid scarf
Red down coat
Green sweatpants
Socks
Black snow boots
White turtleneck sweater

TESS
Tan sweater
Long sleeve t-shirt
Tan pj pants
Socks
Flat shoes
Tan coat
Headscarf

PRESENT
Green hat
Red curly wig
Green bodice with fur collar
Red velvet skirt with green
    petticoat
White petticoat
Red tights
Lace up boots
White fishnet gloves
Toothblack
Tanktop
Hankie

CAROLER #1
Same as above

SARAH
Santa hat
Green "Homeless Helper"
    apron/vest
Black boots
Blue glasses
Red sweatshirt
White turtleneck
Jeans

COSTUMES

ELEANOR #1
 Blue Suit
 Cream blouse
 Blue trouser socks
 Black coat
 Purse/bag
 Black shoes
 Blue socks
 Glasses on a chain

ELEANOR #2
 Santa Jacket
 Santa Pants
 Santa Hat
 Black Boots
 Black Belt
 White Wig
 White Beard on elastic
 Body padding
 White gloves

BOBBY #1
 Glasses
 Red/pink scarf
 Grey tweed coat
 Grey suit jacket
 Tan turtleneck sweater
 Leg warmers
 Grey tights
 Sneakers
 Black fingerless gloves
 Pencils for hair

BOBBY #2
 Blue sweater
 Grey sweatpants
 Socks
 Slippers

BOBBY #3
 Same as Bobby #1
 Black coat
 Dark grey scarf

BOBBY #4
 Same as Bobby #1

CAROLER #1
 Red plaid hat
 Green gloves
 Red plaid scarf
 Red down coat
 Green sweatpants
 Socks
 Black snow boots
 White turtleneck sweater

TESS
 Tan sweater
 Long sleeve t-shirt
 Tan pj pants
 Socks
 Flat shoes
 Tan coat
 Headscarf

PRESENT
 Green hat
 Red curly wig
 Green bodice with fur collar
 Red velvet skirt with green
  petticoat
 White petticoat
 Red tights
 Lace up boots
 White fishnet gloves
 Toothblack
 Tanktop
 Hankie

CAROLER #1
 Same as above

SARAH
 Santa hat
 Green "Homeless Helper"
  apron/vest
 Black boots
 Blue glasses
 Red sweatshirt
 White turtleneck
 Jeans

NURSE
 White scrub top
 White scrub bottoms
 White nurse shoes
 Blue cardigan sweater

SARAH

Same as above

CARLA #1

Green sweater set

Black pants

Black shoes

Wig

Glasses

Wedding ring

NELLIE

Line green sweater

Short red dress

Push up bra

Silver shoes

Red/white stripe stockings

Red bead necklace

Bell earrings

Red wig

Silver bracelets

White leather/fur coat

Assorted silver rings

Headband with springs and
lights

CARLA #2

Green coat

White scarf

White fur hat

Red leather gloves

CAROLER #3

Red Chenille Scarf

White beret

Green Fleece coat

White snow boots

Red/white stripe gloves

Socks

T-shirt

Jeans

ELLIE

Cream blouse

Blue suit

Black shoes

Trench coat

Scarf

Purse

Briefcase

LISA

Red beaded sweater

Black skirt

Black shoes

Pearl necklace

Black bobbed wig

Glasses

CAROLER #3

Same as above

CAROLER #2

Green scarf

Snowflake sweater

Tan cord pants

Black boots

VENDOR

Brown wool hat

Tan Henley

Green flannel shirt

Jeans

Brown work boots

Work gloves

BILL

Khaki pants

Green /blue plaid shirt

Brown loafers

Green sweater

CAROLER #2

Same as above

ANGEL OF DEATH

Long black coat

Black shirt

Black pants

Black platform boots

Sunglasses

Black leather gloves

ELEANOR #1

Blue Suit

Cream blouse

Blue trouser socks

Black coat

Purse/bag

Black shoes
Blue socks
Glasses on a chain

ELEANOR #2

Santa Jacket
Santa Pants
Santa Hat
Black Boots
Black Belt
White Wig
White Beard on elastic
Body padding
White gloves

BOBBY #1

Glasses
Red/pink scarf
Grey tweed coat
Grey suit jacket
Tan turtleneck sweater
Leg warmers
Grey tights
Sneakers
Black fingerless gloves
Pencils for hair

BOBBY #2

Blue sweater
Grey sweatpants
Socks
Slippers

BOBBY #3

Same as Bobby #1
Black coat
Dark grey scarf

BOBBY #4

Same as Bobby #1

CAROLER #1

Red plaid hat
Green gloves
Red plaid scarf
Red down coat
Green sweatpants
Socks
Black snow boots
White turtleneck sweater

TESS

Tan sweater
Long sleeve t-shirt
Tan pj pants
Socks
Flat shoes
Tan coat
Headscarf

PRESENT

Green hat
Red curly wig
Green bodice with fur collar
Red velvet skirt with green
    petticoat
White petticoat
Red tights
Lace up boots
White fishnet gloves
Toothblack
Tanktop
Hankie

CAROLER #1

Same as above

SARAH

Santa hat
Green "Homeless Helper"
    apron/vest
Black boots
Blue glasses
Red sweatshirt
White turtleneck
Jeans

NURSE

White scrub top
White scrub bottoms
White nurse shoes
Blue cardigan sweater

SARAH

Same as above

CARLA #1

Green sweater set
Black pants
Black shoes
Wig

Glasses
Wedding ring

NELLIE
Line green sweater
Short red dress
Push up bra
Silver shoes
Red/white stripe stockings
Red bead necklace
Bell earrings
Red wig
Silver bracelets
White leather/fur coat
Assorted silver rings
Headband with springs and lights

CARLA #2
Green coat
White scarf
White fur hat
Red leather gloves

CAROLER #3
Red Chenille Scarf
White beret
Green Fleece coat
White snow boots
Red/white stripe gloves
Socks
T-shirt
Jeans

ELLIE
Cream blouse
Blue suit
Black shoes
Trench coat
Scarf
Purse
Briefcase

LISA
Red beaded sweater
Black skirt
Black shoes
Pearl necklace
Black bobbed wig

Glasses

CAROLER #3
Same as above

CAROLER #2
Green scarf
Snowflake sweater
Tan cord pants
Black boots

VENDOR
Brown wool hat
Tan Henley
Green flannel shirt
Jeans
Brown work boots
Work gloves

BILL
Khaki pants
Green /blue plaid shirt
Brown loafers
Green sweater

CAROLER #2
Same as above

ANGEL OF DEATH
Long black coat
Black shirt
Black pants
Black platform boots
Sunglasses
Black leather gloves
Black belt with skull buckle

YOUNG PHIL
White button down shirt
Red sweater
Grey slacks
Grey socks
Brown loafers
Grey down coat
Blue gloves
Giants Hat

TIMMY #1
PJ pants
Socks
T shirt

TIMMY #2
Red Christmas sweater
Jeans
Black shoes
Jean jacket
Red/grey hat
Black gloves

BEN
Santa hat
Green "Homeless Helper"
    apron/vest
Black boots
brown glasses
Red sweatshirt
White turtleneck
Jeans

JOHN MISTELHOUSE
Black striped coat with grey
    fur collar
Grey/brown scarf
Grey suit pants
Brown/grey tie
White button shirt
Belt
Black leather gloves
Socks
Black shoes
Glasses
Grey wool hat

ROBERT
Tan trench coat
Green/gold/red scarf
Tan check suit blazer
Olive green dress pants
Cream turtleneck
Belt
Brown gloves
Brown loafers
Watch

GRAVEDIGGER
Black rubber coat
Brown snow hat with ear flaps
Green fingerless gloves
Green rubber boots

Brown overalls
Tan long sleeve t-shirt

JOHN MISTELHOUSE
same as above

MARLEY #1
Light grey suit with silver
    pinstripes
Light grey shirt
Light grey tie
Grey socks
Horns that light up
Belt
Light grey pocket square

MARLEY #2
Black overcoat
Black Homburg hat
Black pants
Black socks
Black shoes
Black gloves
Scarf

BENSON
Brown overcoat
Wool hat
Glasses
Grey wig
Grey moustache
Green scarf

CAROLER #4
Red coat
Green knit hat
Brown glasses
Green scarf
Jeans
Brown snow boots
Socks
Green gloves
Red sweater

PAST
With an Ancient Mongolian
    style grey/blue hat with
    fur edge
Long double breasted blue
    wool coat with Mandarin

collar
Tall black boots
Black leggings
Round silver glasses

JUAN

Tight Black shirt
Full Red pants
Red socks
Long toed shoes
Red belt
Gold chain
Black scarf with fringe
Black windowpane jacket
Gold rings
Bracelet

PHIL

Giants cap
Red scarf
Brown gloves
Dark red sweater
Khaki pants
Tan socks
Brown loafers
Belt
White button down shirt

PHIL #2

Remove coat, hat and gloves
Add sports jacket

PHIL #3

Black coat
Dark scarf
Black tie
Black slacks
Black shoes

PHIL #4

Same as #1
Christmas sweater

PROPS

Eleanor's computer
Bobbie's computer
[2] phone intercom
desk accessories
desk accessories
dish of chocolate kisses
[2]framed photo of Timmy
bell
bottle of water
purrel
[several] files
[several] files
purse
change purse
large briefcase
scheduling book
Misslehouse Memo
Christmas cookie tin
burnt cookies
Christmas donations boot
washcloth
cup of coffee
scarf
purse
Forbes magazine
office keys
Christmas tree 1
wallet
cash
Purse
candy cane
wheelchair
Christmas card 1
purse
Christmas card 2
business card
Tess' coat
briefcase
Ring box
engagement ring
flask
4 wine Glasses

Christmas tree 2
files
plate of cookies [2]
glass of milk
Christmas present
cell phone
smutty girls magazine
pencil cup
nail file
compact
lipstick
box of wine
clipboard
eviction notice
Christmas card
flowers
shovel
Christmas cookies in tin
newspaper
cell phone
large garment bag
platter of Christmas cookies
large bowl of cider
cups
cash
big red bag full of gifts
Nintendo Wii box
envelope and card
envelope and card
letter rolled up, tied w/red ribbon
small unwrapped ring box
Tess' engagement ring
envelope and card
blank check
old Christmas card

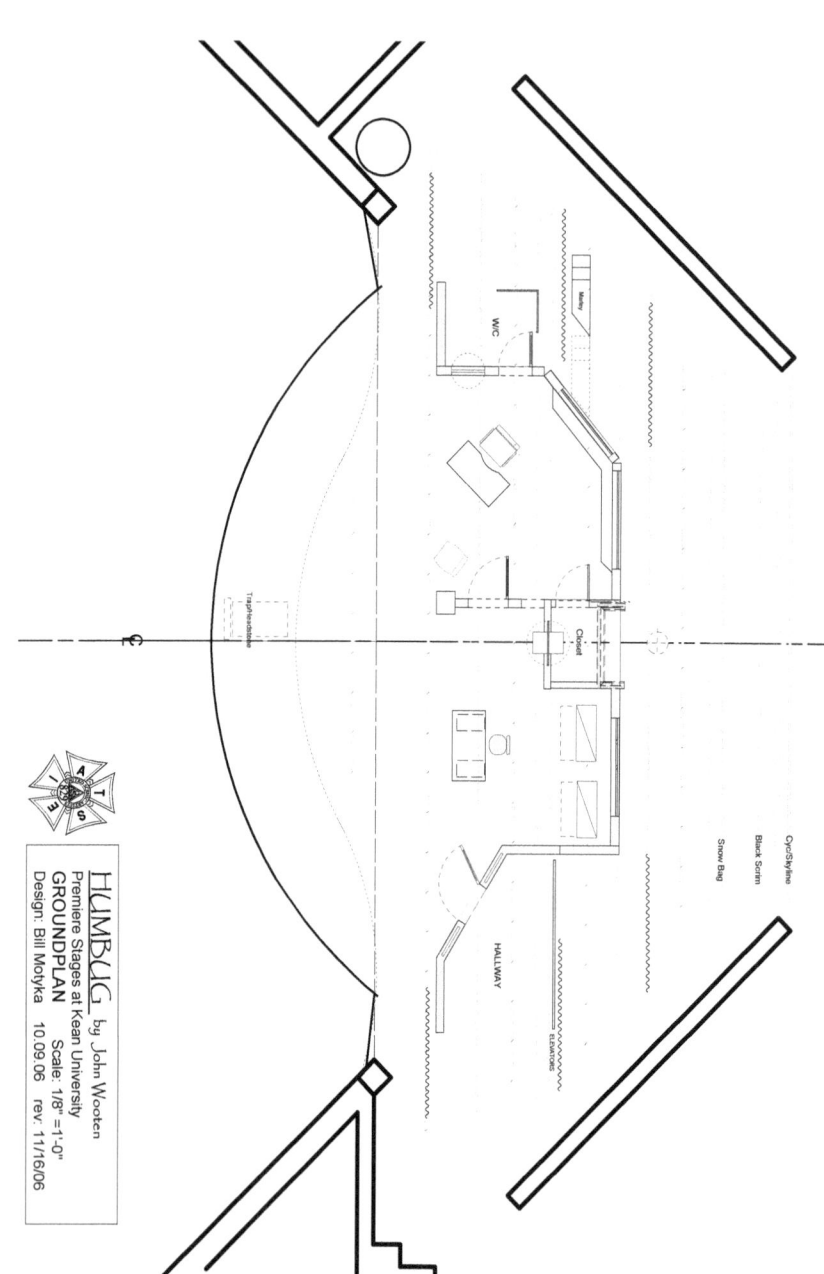

From the Reviews of
HUMBUG...

"Wooten has indeed concocted a comedy that puts a great deal of delicious nonsense into Charles Dickens' most famous story...a multitude of laughs"
– *The Newark Star-Ledger*

"*Humbug* is full of humor, warmth...a must see addition to the list of holiday classics"
– *The Home News Tribune*

"A witty, timely, poignant script interspersed with upbeat Christmas carols and a timeless message of caring"
– *The Westfield Leader*

"Wooten has nicely shaped his fast paced and lively conceit into a 75-minute play while finding clever modern day equivalents for most of Dickens' characters and situations, and even adding a principal thread of his own...pleasant, bright Christmas entertainment for the entire family"
– *Talkin' Broadway*

"The play is for the entire family. Adults will be moved by it, and it would make for a fascinating introduction to live theatre for five-year-olds and up"
– *Union Leader*

OTHER TITLES AVAILABLE FROM SAMUEL FRENCH

THE OFFICE PLAYS
Two full length plays by Adam Bock

THE RECEPTIONIST
Comedy / 2m., 2f. Interior

At the start of a typical day in the Northeast Office, Beverly deals effortlessly with ringing phones and her colleague's romantic troubles. But the appearance of a charming rep from the Central Office disrupts the friendly routine. And as the true nature of the company's business becomes apparent, The Receptionist raises disquieting, provocative questions about the consequences of complicity with evil.

"...Mr. Bock's poisoned Post-it note of a play." - *New York Times*

"Bock's intense initial focus on the routine goes to the heart of *The Receptionist's* pointed, painfully timely allegory... elliptical, provocative play..."
- *Time Out New York*

THE THUGS
Comedy / 2m, 6f / Interior

The Obie Award winning dark comedy about work, thunder and the mysterious things that are happening on the 9th floor of a big law firm. When a group of temps try to discover the secrets that lurk in the hidden crevices of their workplace, they realize they would rather believe in gossip and rumors than face dangerous realities.

"Bock starts you off giggling, but leaves you with a chill."
- *Time Out New York*

"... a delightfully paranoid little nightmare that is both more chillingly realistic and pointedly absurd than anything John Grisham ever dreamed up."
- *New York Times*

OTHER TITLES AVAILABLE FROM SAMUEL FRENCH

A VERY MERRY UNAUTHORIZED
CHILDREN'S SCIENTOLOGY PAGEANT
Kyle Jarrow

Musical / 5m, 5f (Doubling possible) / Interior
A jubilant cast of children celebrate the controversial religion in uplifting pageantry and song. The actual teachings of The Church of Scientology are explained and dissected against the candy-colored backdrop of a traditional nativity play. Pageant is a musical biography of the life of L. Ron Hubbard, with child-friendly explanations of Hubbard's notion of the divided mind (embodied by the lovely identical twins Emma and Sophie Whitfield in matching brain outfits) and a device called the e-meter (or electropsychometer), used to monitor the human psyche, which is demonstrated by stick puppets. Grade school children, portraying Tom Cruise, Kirstie Alley, John Travolta, and other less starry Scientologists, brings the controversial Church of Scientology to jubilant life in story and song.

www.ingramcontent.com/pod-product-compliance
Lightning Source LLC
Chambersburg PA
CBHW070639120726
47909CB00004B/1506